D0405756

CHARLIE NUMB3RS
and the man in the moon

Also by Ben Mezrich

Bringing Down the Mouse

CHARLIE NUMB3RS

and the man in the moon

BEN and TONYA MEZRICH

Simon & Schuster Books for Young Readers

NEW YORK   LONDON   TORONTO   SYDNEY   NEW DELHI

SIMON & SCHUSTER BOOKS FOR YOUNG READERS
An imprint of Simon & Schuster Children's Publishing Division
1230 Avenue of the Americas, New York, New York 10020
This book is a work of fiction. Any references to historical events, real people, or real places are used fictitiously. Other names, characters, places, and events are products of the author's imagination, and any resemblance to actual events or places or persons, living or dead, is entirely coincidental.
SIMON & SCHUSTER BOOKS FOR YOUNG READERS
is a trademark of Simon & Schuster, Inc.
For information about special discounts for bulk purchases, please contact Simon & Schuster Special Sales at 1-866-506-1949 or business@simonandschuster.com.
The Simon & Schuster Speakers Bureau can bring authors to your live event. For more information or to book an event, contact the Simon & Schuster Speakers Bureau at 1-866-248-3049 or visit our website at www.simonspeakers.com.
Jacket design by Krista Vossen
Interior design by Hilary Zarycky
The text for this book was set in Life LT Std.
Manufactured in the United States of America
1017 FFG
First Edition
2 4 6 8 10 9 7 5 3 1
Library of Congress Cataloging-in-Publication Data
Names: Mezrich, Ben, 1969– author. | Mezrich, Tonya, author.
Title: Charlie Numbers and the man in the moon / Ben & Tonya Mezrich.
Description: First edition. | New York : Simon & Schuster Books for Young Readers, [2017] | Summary: When sixth-grade mathematical genius Charlie Lewis is recruited to recover moon rocks taken from NASA's vaults, the Whiz Kids enter a paper airplane contest hosted by the suspect's company.
Identifiers: LCCN 2016056388| ISBN 9781481448475 (hardback) | ISBN 9781481448499 (eBook)
Subjects: | CYAC: Mathematics—Fiction. | Genius—Fiction. | Moon rocks—Fiction. | Paper airplanes—Fiction. | Contests—Fiction. | Mystery and detective stories. | BISAC: JUVENILE FICTION / Social Issues / Peer Pressure. | JUVENILE FICTION / Social Issues / Friendship. | JUVENILE FICTION / Humorous Stories.
Classification: LCC PZ7.M5753 Ch 2017 | DDC [Fic]—dc23
LC record available at https://lccn.loc.gov/2016056388

To our little angels, Asher and Arya—
you are our beacons on this jet plane of life

ACKNOWLEDGMENTS

David Gale, thank you for wholeheartedly getting behind this second book in the Charlie Numbers series and giving me a chance to coauthor it with my husband. As a steadfast editor with a stellar team, especially Amanda Ramirez and Jenica Nasworthy at S&S Books for Young Readers, you have made all of this possible. To our agents Eric Simonoff and Matt Snyder, we are forever grateful to you. To my dear friend Titi Dang, thank you for your never-ending kindness and support. Ellen Pompeo and Chris Ivery, we are thrilled and excited to be working with the whole team at Calamity Jane, especially Laura Holstein, to bring this series to the screen. A special thanks to my parents, Ron and Fu-mei Chen, for giving me the foundation to live and carry out my dreams, and to my three wonderful, supportive siblings, Sonya, Oliver, and Tree.

And most important of all, thank you to my love, my all—Ben, for giving me two amazing children and one pug, and for believing in me and giving me the strength and motivation to bring Charlie's adventure to life.

—Tonya Mezrich

There's a fine line between flying and falling.
The only real difference is what happens when
you hit the ground. . . .

TEN MINUTES PAST NOON on a Thursday in late January, and Charlie Lewis was trying to figure out how everything in his life had gone so utterly wrong. He wasn't in school. He wasn't at home. Heck, he wasn't even in Massachusetts. He was, in fact, crouched low in the egg-shaped cockpit of a one-hundred-year-old, rickety wooden biplane hanging fifty feet above the vast and open main atrium of the Smithsonian Institution's Air and Space Museum, trying not to think about the long drop down to the unforgiving marble floor below.

The more he trembled at his predicament, the more the biplane quivered and swayed beneath his weight.

Above him, he could see the single, coiled wire leading from the center of the biplane's upper wing to the stabilizing pipes crisscrossing the arched ceiling of the atrium. He had no idea how strong the coil was, or how it was attached to the pipes, but he knew that the wire was the only thing between him and a harrowing plummet down, down, down—

"There's nowhere to go, kid. Game over."

The voice came from Charlie's left, and not far away. He didn't need to look to know that his pursuer was getting closer by the minute. Each time Charlie blinked, he could see the man in his memory: square face beneath a frighteningly perfect crew cut, oversize muscles bulging beneath a dark tailored suit, sweat stains seeping through the collar of an ever-present white dress shirt that always seemed to be two sizes too small. From the sound of the man's voice, Charlie guessed the man had already crawled halfway across the iron catwalk that ran beneath the suspension pipes—which meant he was just a few yards away from the biplane now, and getting closer by the second.

Game over. Charlie finally forced himself to glance over the edge of the swaying cockpit, and found himself staring straight down those fifty feet to the atrium floor below. He was immediately hit by a wave of vertigo but fought through the dizzying sensation. The main floor was fairly crowded for the middle of the day: maybe two dozen people, mostly tourists. Bright colored sweatshirts, baseball hats, mothers pushing carriages, tour guides corralling charges. From so high up, they all looked like little dolls, the type Charlie had never really played with as a kid. He'd been more interested in puzzles, graphs, cards—anything even vaguely scientific. As much as he disliked the nickname that had been following him around since he'd inadvertently aced a test geared toward high school freshmen when he was in fourth grade, "Numbers" really did fit him. At twelve, he was already flirting with college-level mathematics; sometimes his teachers at Nagassack Middle School in Newton, Massachusetts, asked *him* for help with their syllabi. Even so, as smart as he was supposed to be, Charlie seemed to have a knack for getting himself into situations like this.

Well, maybe not like this. The biplane jerked beneath Charlie as the man on the catwalk moved another foot closer, and Charlie gasped, his fingers tightening against the edge of the cockpit. The vertigo doubled in intensity, and Charlie willed himself to focus, pinning his gaze to one of the iconic displays on the ground floor of the museum—directly beneath the biplane, planted on a swath of orange-red carpet that extended from the glass entrance at the front to the stairs leading up to the various levels and exhibits.

Even from above, Lindbergh's *Spirit of St. Louis* was inspiring; covered in silvery fabric, with its bulbous gas tank up front, the modified Ryan Airlines model had been the first airplane to be flown solo and nonstop across the Atlantic in 1927, completing the trip from New York to Paris in thirty-three and a half hours, touching down at Le Bourget Field in front of an audience of more than one hundred thousand. At the time, the plane had signified one of mankind's greatest accomplishments. Now it sat kitty-corner to the rust-colored Apollo space capsule that had carried astronauts Buzz Aldrin, Neil Armstrong, and Michael Collins home from the moon in July of 1969, in the center of the country's largest museum dedicated to flight—fifty feet below a swaying biplane and a terrified, too-smart-for-his-own-good sixth grader, who was about to do something incredibly stupid.

Charlie pulled his gaze upward from the *Spirit of St. Louis* and the space capsule, pausing when he reached the museum's second-level balcony, twenty feet in front of the biplane's propeller, but still a good thirty feet below.

It didn't take him long to spot Jeremy "Diapers" Draper, his best friend and fellow sixth grader from Nagassack Middle. With his bright shock of red hair, stretched-out frame, and stringy arms and legs, Jeremy was hard to miss. Even pressed up against the second-floor glass railing, trying to hide himself in a crowd of raucous high schoolers in matching gray athletic jerseys, Jeremy stood out. Bean Pole, Scarecrow, Pipe Cleaner—Charlie's best friend had endured a cornucopia of nicknames tied to his unique physical characteristics, before the middle-school mob had settled on Diapers. Had Jeremy's mother not mistakenly filled his backpack with his baby sister's disposables, and had Jeremy managed not to trip during lunch hour in the last week of fifth grade and spill said backpack all over the lunchroom, in full view of the entire middle school—he'd have been Scarecrow or Pipe Cleaner until the day he shipped himself off to college.

Diapers was a tough label to wear in the *Lord of the Flies* environment of Nagassack Middle, but at the moment, Charlie would have happily traded nicknames with his friend, if doing so could somehow have magically transported him from the cockpit of the biplane to the safety of the Smithsonian's second-floor balcony.

Unfortunately, Charlie knew, there was no such thing as magic. Only math. But sometimes math could be a sort of magic; at the moment, with the crew cut bearing down on him and the biplane dangling beneath his weight, Charlie had only one choice—he was going to have to use math to do the most magical thing mankind had ever achieved.

He was going to have to use math to make himself fly.

Charlie took a deep breath, then reached behind himself in the cockpit and unzipped the backpack that was hanging from a strap around his left shoulder. He retrieved a pair of gardening shears then quickly zipped it shut. He held them at arm's length, inspecting the sharpness of the blades, the way the light glanced off the smooth, almost glassy metal. Then he rose to a near standing position in the cockpit and raised the shears toward the coiled wire that held the biplane in place.

"Kid, are you nuts?" the crew cut hissed from just a few feet away on the catwalk.

But Charlie was already gone, his mind lost in a swirl of calculations: The length of the biplane's wings and the amount of air they would displace. The volume of the atrium and the distance to the second-floor balcony. The angle of descent and the weight of the plane's wooden frame, fabric covering, and propeller.

The tensile strength and physical diameter of the coiled wire that held the biplane to the ceiling and the torque-based cutting power of a pair of steel gardening sheers.

"Kid, don't do it. Kid!"

But Charlie was already reaching for the wire.

Newton, Massachusetts, Ten Days Earlier

"BAKING SODA, SALT, WATER, some vinegar, a little milk for color, and good old-fashioned playground dirt. I think we're in business."

Charlie watched Crystal Mueller as she carefully placed the supplies, one after another, across the picnic table in the back corner of the playground. First, the two bright orange cartons of Arm & Hammer that Charlie had just pulled out of his backpack, along with the milk and vinegar. Then the canister of salt that their diminutive friend, Kentaro Mori, had borrowed from the lunchroom ten minutes earlier—when the recess bell had first rung, signaling the beginning of the brief twenty minutes of shared freedom before fifth-period English began. Followed by the plastic pitcher of water that Marion Tuttle had siphoned from the water fountain behind the swings at the other end of the playground; the chubby redhead had needed to unscrew the side panel of the fountain to reach the water pipes—the fountain hadn't worked properly since an eighth grader had tried to use the poor device as a football tackling dummy two months earlier. And finally, a plastic bucket full of moist dirt that spring-limbed, giraffe-height redhead Jeremy Draper had dredged out of the flower bed that ran behind the seesaw. The dirt had been the most difficult to procure, since the seesaw was the kind of prime playground real estate that attracted the sort of sixth graders who wore Little League baseball uniforms to school, even when they didn't have a game scheduled until the following afternoon. But Jeremy had somehow dug enough dirt to satisfy Crystal without catching anyone's attention. Which, for the most part, was the daily goal of kids like Charlie, Jeremy, Kentaro, Marion, and Crystal.

Just get through the day without catching any unwanted attention.

"So what the heck does salt, baking soda, water, and dirt have to do with Utah?" Jeremy asked as he stuck a pipe-cleaner finger into the dirt before Crystal shooed him away. "And how is this going to help us with our geography project?"

"Have you ever *been* to Utah, Jeremy?" she asked.

Jeremy shook his head. Crystal rolled her eyes, then turned to Charlie.

"Did you bring the ceramic casserole pan?"

Charlie dug into his backpack again, retrieving one of his mom's baking pans.

"You didn't say anything about ceramic. I think this is aluminum. Is that going to be a problem?"

"Not for me. But the salt's going to wreck it."

Charlie was fairly certain that Crystal could burn a hole in the pan and his mother would never notice. A double PhD in virology and biology, his mother was usually at the university until well after Charlie was in bed, lights out; she hadn't cooked anything in the kitchen in as long as he could remember. She wasn't going to miss the casserole pan any more than Charlie's dad—an engineer and MIT professor with multiple PhDs of his own—was going to notice the missing battery-powered hot plate Charlie had borrowed from the camping supplies that had been collecting dust in a corner of their home garage.

"I think an A is worth a ruined casserole pan," Charlie said, retrieving the hot plate and placing it next to the other items on the picnic table.

Crystal smiled as she went at her work, attacking the

boxes of baking soda with her fingernails. Of course, As weren't a rare commodity for any of Charlie's group of friends: the Whiz Kids—a nickname that Charlie's parents had coined for the group, who had a combined IQ well in the stratosphere. Kentaro, despite his miniature size, was a linguistic giant, a wizard with anything that contained letters and sounds. Marion—though in a constant life-or-death struggle with allergies to just about everything organic that lived on land, sea, or air—was a master artist. Jeremy, like Charlie himself, had mad math skills and had been acing AP math and science classes since he'd turned eleven. And Crystal might as well have had her own PhD in geology. Her knowledge of rocks far surpassed most of the teachers at Nagassack Middle School.

Crafting a salt flat out of common household items for a report on Utah was decidedly simpler than the working model of the Hoover Dam they'd built a year earlier for their report on Nevada, or the HO-scale diorama of Niagara Falls—with running water—they'd created the year before that. But Charlie and Jeremy had been catching up on missed schoolwork since their recent trip to Incredo Land, the amusement park in Florida; a sort of "working" vacation during which they, along with a group of other sixth and seventh graders, had used their mathematical skills to take down a series of carnival games. Charlie hadn't seen the others, the mysterious Finn or the oddly beguiling Sam, since he'd been back, except in passing—hallways before class, far corner of the lunchroom—but he'd had too much on his plate to really notice. The Utah geology project was last on a long list of assignments with deadlines coming fast; he was only glad that it was a group project, rather than something he'd have to complete all on his own.

Behind her thick glasses, Crystal gazed at the lines on a Pyrex measuring cup, pouring in just enough of the salt and leveling it off at the two-cup mark. Then she shifted toward the casserole pan.

"This should be the exact right proportion. Mix this in with the water; I'll start heating the dirt."

Charlie took the cup from her hands as she turned toward the hot plate. He was about to pour the salt into the pan, when out of the corner of his eyes he saw a flash of motion. He just had time to make out the shape of a football, flying in a perfect spiral toward him—when he felt the hard thud of leather against his chest, and the measuring cup went flying into the air. Kosher salt billowed in a blizzard around his head, and when the salt cleared, Charlie was bent over, catching his breath, staring down at a pair of scuffed high-top sneakers. Sneakers so large they could only belong to one person.

Dylan Wigglesworth. Double the size of an average sixth grader, with thick dark hair sticking out from beneath a Little League baseball hat and arms the size of train pistons. The thick-necked behemoth motioned to his two henchman—Liam Anthony and Dusty Bickle, curly-haired thugs in matching striped jerseys—to find the football, which had ricocheted off of Charlie and was now sitting squarely in the casserole pan.

"What are you doing Num-*bers*? Baking brownies for the teachers? Running low on big fat butt kisses?"

Charlie could feel his face turning red as he picked up the measuring cup. Dylan never seemed to tire of torturing the Whiz Kids: tripping them in the hallways, throwing food at them in the lunchroom. The teachers at Nagassack mostly turned a blind eye to the bullying; as long as Dylan kept it out of the classrooms, the teachers figured it was kids being kids. Which meant the Whiz Kids had to deal with it on their own, in any way they could. Usually, their tried-and-true methods were staying out of sight or running for the hills. Neither seemed an option at the moment.

"It's just a geology project. Nothing exciting, Dylan."

Dylan's foxlike eyes shrunk as he grabbed one of

the boxes of baking soda and shook it up and down. The white powder puffed into a huge cloud in the air, billowing down to the pile of salt on the ground. "Let it snow!"

Liam and Dusty howled in delight. Charlie felt his anger growing—he had to do something, fast—but the simple physics of the situation made standing up for himself incredibly dangerous. Dylan was stronger than all of the Whiz Kids put together, not even factoring in his two sidekicks. Charlie's only chance was to use his brain, not his body. And he had to work fast. He could see the crowd of sixth graders growing behind Dylan; they were attracting a heck of an audience. Brains to trump body—*or maybe there was a way to use both.*

Charlie glanced at the football, which Liam had retrieved from the casserole pan. Then he looked toward the supplies still lined up behind Crystal on the picnic table: what was left of the salt, one remaining box of baking soda, vinegar, milk, water. The hot plate, already heating up, on the table between Jeremy and Kentaro. A thought stirred inside Charlie's head. Could it work? Could he pull it off?

He made a sudden decision and pointed toward Liam and the football.

"Dylan, I can see that baking's not really your thing.

So, how about a little football-throwing contest—me against you?"

Dylan stared at him, as a hush moved through the crowd of onlookers.

"You've got to be kidding. I could throw you farther than you could throw that football."

"I'm sure you're right. Should be an easy win for you. So you're in? Unless, of course, you're chicken."

Charlie regretted the words the minute he'd said them. Bright red cauliflowers spread across Dylan's cheeks, and for a brief second it looked like he was going to throw a punch. But even through his rage, Dylan could sense the change in the playground air— now almost every sixth grader within a hundred yards was watching, waiting to see how it all played out.

"It's your funeral, Numbers. I'll beat you in the contest, and then I'll *beat* you in real life. How about you throw first?"

Dylan nodded at Liam, who tossed the football in a high arc toward Charlie. Charlie missed the catch, and the ball landed in the mud between his feet. As he bent to pick it up, he signaled Crystal and Jeremy in for a quick huddle.

"Are you nuts?" Jeremy hissed. "You can't throw a football ten feet. Dylan's going to crush you."

Charlie aimed a surreptitious finger toward the picnic table.

"Crystal. Two tablespoons of vinegar. Two cups of milk. Into the casserole pan, and get it on the hot plate as fast as you can."

Crystal looked at him for a beat, and then a smile flashed across her lips. Without a word, she turned and headed for the supplies. Jeremy watched her go, a puzzled look on his face. Charlie snapped a finger, getting his friend's attention.

"Find another bowl, fast. Whatever's left of the baking soda, mix it with water. When Crystal's done with the hot plate, filter what she's got—use a towel if you can find one, if not, a big leaf might work. Mix what's left all together. And then start praying."

Charlie grabbed the football and rose, giving Jeremy a little push toward the rest of the supplies. Then he crossed slowly toward where Dylan was standing, pawlike hands on his hips. Dylan pointed toward the high fence that separated the playground from the soccer fields.

"The fence is about twenty yards away. You couldn't hit it in your dreams."

Charlie squared his shoulders toward the fence, trying to control the tremble moving through his limbs.

The football felt huge in his small hand, the rough leather too taut for his fingers to get a really good grip. He could hear the titters of laughter from the crowd behind him; there had to be twenty kids watching.

To his right, he could hear Crystal and Jeremy working with the supplies. He knew it was going to be tight—if this was going to work, every second was going to count—but he couldn't stall any longer. If the crowd got restless, Dylan would give them a show and Charlie would be the object sailing toward that fence.

"Okay, here goes," Charlie muttered. Then he cocked his arm as far back as he could and let the football fly.

Even he had to admit it was a pretty pathetic arc. The football wobbled as it flew through the air, barely clearing the metal bar at the top of the swing set. Then it plummeted to the grass, maybe fifteen feet from where he and Dylan were standing.

"Even worse than I'd expected," Dylan laughed, in concert with the cackles from the audience.

Charlie headed to retrieve the football. He tried to ignore the laughter and catcalls coming his way. He moved as slowly as he felt he could get away with, giving Crystal and Jeremy as much time as he could. When he grabbed the ball, he glanced toward the picnic table and saw Crystal pouring the now-heated contents of the casserole pan through a handful of napkins from the lunchroom into an upside-down Frisbee balanced in Jeremy's hands.

Perfect. Charlie tucked the football under his arm and headed back toward Dylan. He'd made it about halfway when he allowed himself to stumble—fumbling the football directly toward where Jeremy and Crystal were standing. As Dylan and the watching crowd laughed even harder, Charlie rushed after the football, signaling Jeremy with his eyes as he went.

Jeremy took two steps forward, the Frisbee out in front of him. Then he, too, stumbled, his long legs connecting, and he dropped the Frisbee, right on top of the football.

"You and Diapers should open up a circus," Dylan howled. "Tweedledee and Tweedledum."

Charlie reached the football and picked it up from beneath the Frisbee, careful to hold it by its underside. The top of the football was now covered in brownish-white clumps. As Charlie carried it toward Dylan, he did his best to shake the clumps off.

"It's kind of dirty," he apologized. "You want to get a different ball?"

Dylan yanked the football out of Charlie's hands.

"I could beat your throw with a bowling ball. Get out of the way, Numbers."

He turned to face the fence, cocked his arm back like an NFL quarterback about to win the Super Bowl, and then threw his arm forward with all his might.

—And nothing happened. The ball clung to his open palm, the leather stuck to his skin by the white and yellow clumps. Dylan's eyes widened. He started to curse, violently shaking his hand up and down—and finally the football came loose, tumbling to the dirt right in front of his shoes.

"Looks like about six inches," Jeremy said, pointing to where the football had landed. "You want us to get the measuring tape? I'm pretty sure Charlie has you beat."

There was a pause—and then the entire audience of sixth graders burst out in laughter. Dylan looked down at his hand, covered in Charlie's homemade glue. Then a vein rose beneath the skin of his forehead, his cheeks turning a dangerous shade of purple.

"Numbers," he growled.

Charlie took a step back, his heart pounding, a mixture of pride and terror rising in his chest. He knew he was poking a lion with a stick, but beating Dylan, even through a little bit of playground chemistry, felt good.

What was going to come next, though, wasn't going to feel good at all.

Charlie was about to turn and start running when a loud, adult voice rang through the playground.

"Charlie Lewis! You've got some visitors who need to have a word with you!"

Mrs. Fowler, Charlie's fifth-period English teacher, was standing by the open glass doors leading into the lunchroom. Her dowdy, compact four-and-a-half-foot frame was dwarfed by the two figures standing on either side of her: a man and woman, both in dark business suits. The woman had on thick sunglasses and a wide-brimmed hat; her features were sharp, almost knifelike, and her lips seemed as thin as the edge of a piece of paper. The man was large and athletic, muscles rippling beneath what was visible of his white shirt. He had a crew cut that reminded Charlie of one of his old G.I. Joe action figures.

"Hurry up please," Mrs. Fowler continued. "Ten minutes until the fifth-period bell, and I don't want any of you missing the start of today's pop quiz." A mass groan moved across the playground as the crowd dispersed. Charlie reached for his backpack, then started toward Fowler and the two strangers. As he passed Dylan, the bigger kid leaned toward him, whispering under his breath. "We'll finish this later," he hissed.

Charlie brushed past him as fast as he could. He had no idea who the suited man and woman were, or what they wanted with him, but he was certain they had just saved his hide. Even so, beating Dylan in front of an audience had been worth it—even if it meant Charlie would be watching his back for the rest of the school year.

Maybe he'd get lucky. Maybe the two strangers were there to spirit him and the Whiz Kids away from Nagassack long enough for Dylan to move on to other targets. Judging from the look on Dylan's face, a think tank in the Arctic Circle might be just far enough.

3

FOR THE MOMENT, UNFORTUNATELY, the back corner of the lunchroom would have to do.

Charlie's sneakers squeaked against the polished linoleum floor as he followed the two strangers toward a metal table in the rear of the vast room. Save for the three of them, the place was nearly empty; the seventh graders had already moved on to their next class, and Charlie's own grade would be outside on the playground for at least another nine minutes—more if the easily confused Mrs. Fowler had miscalculated the time to the fifth-period bell, which happened more often than not. Other than a few hairnet-capped lunch ladies lingering near the buffet at the front of the room, the place was an empty cave, reeking of chlorinated cleaning supplies and the hint of the remnants of overcooked sloppy joes emanating from the stuffed trash barrels running along the far wall.

When they reached the metal table, the woman gestured for Charlie to take a seat directly across from her. Charlie laid his backpack on the floor by his feet, then watched as the man placed a briefcase between them. The briefcase looked to be plated in steel, with two latches at the top.

Without a word, without taking off her sunglasses or removing her hat, the woman flicked at the latches with her fingers, opening the top of the case. She removed a pair of white gloves from the interior, pulling them on. Then she retrieved a glass vial from an area of cushy foam padding at the center of the case.

She held the vial in front of Charlie. The glass was thick and nearly opaque; Charlie could see some sort of small object inside but couldn't make out any details.

"My name is Anastasia Federov," the woman said. "You don't know me, but I was one of your dad's students a number of years ago, at MIT. This is my associate, Mr. Porter. And we're here because we need your help."

Charlie stared at his own reflection in the woman's sunglasses. Up close, her lips seemed even thinner, if that was possible—like a crack in a windowpane. Her cheeks were tan, and the wisps of hair that hung down from beneath her hat were fine and exceedingly blond. If Charlie had to guess, the woman was in her thirties. Which meant if what she was saying was true, she had been a student of his dad's at least ten years earlier. Since his dad had been a tenured professor at MIT for his entire adult life, he'd probably had thousands of students. But that didn't explain what she was doing at Nagassack, or what she wanted with Charlie.

"My help? I'm just a kid. What could I possibly help you with?"

Anastasia glanced at her partner, who was as still and silent and stony as his icy-blue eyes. Then she leaned closer over the table, lowering her voice.

"Two words: rocket propulsion."

For a brief moment, her response seemed like it had come right out of left field. Certainly, his dad had taught many engineering classes that included the science behind rocket flight; Charlie had sat in on dozens of them over the years, awed by the blackboard-length calculations that went into the design of rocket engines and the chemical properties of the fuel that launched them into the sky. But what did that have to do with him?

And then he remembered. It had to have been

two summers ago, when Charlie had just turned ten. Just before bed, he'd watched part of a show with his father on National Geographic about the Space Race— detailing the incredible efforts of the engineers who had first managed to get a man on the moon, nearly fifty years ago. Charlie had been so excited by the program, he had spent the entire night under his covers with a flashlight, calculating formulas—force, energy, lift, velocity—to try to mimic a small part of what had gone into that great accomplishment. The next day, he'd dashed off a ten-page paper on the subject. His father had been so proud of what he'd done, he'd entered the paper into a science blog contest at the university. The paper hadn't won anything, but Charlie's young age had impressed the judges enough to get him an honorable mention in the MIT school newspaper.

Two years later, Charlie hadn't imagined that a paper he'd written as a ten-year-old could have attracted the attention of anyone outside of his circle of family and friends. Especially anyone who wore suits to visit a middle school or carried a briefcase plated in steel.

"Who are you, exactly?" Charlie asked, his nerves rising. "You're obviously not a student anymore. Why would you be interested in what a kid thinks about rocket propulsion?"

"We work for NASA," Anastasia said.

NASA. Even the name of the place took Charlie's breath away. The National Aeronautics and Space Administration was the organization responsible for the US space program, current and past. It was funded and run by the government, a haven for the best scientists in the world. The very people who had first put a man on the moon.

"So you're engineers?" Charlie asked. "You build spaceships?"

"Not exactly."

The woman looked at her partner again, who remained as still as ever. The man looked like he'd been chiseled right out of marble—with all the personality of a statue. Even so, Charlie's excitement was growing. He'd always dreamed of visiting NASA—maybe even one day, when he was older, being a part of the team of scientists who worked at the organization, creating the next generation of space vehicles. But he never, in his wildest dreams, imagined that NASA would come looking for him.

"What does that mean? You're not scientists?"

Instead of responding, Anastasia tapped the glass vial in front of her with one of her gloved hands. The object inside shifted, coming closer to the glass—and

Charlie saw that it was some sort of tiny rock. Rough and pockmarked, with flecks of reflective material that, even through the thick glass, flashed beneath the lunchroom's fluorescent lights.

"Do you know what this is?" Anastasia asked.

Charlie shook his head. Through the sunglasses, he couldn't tell if the woman was looking at him or the vial.

"This is one of the most valuable objects on earth." She paused for a beat, to let that sink in. "A moon rock. The rarest of all rocks, brought back by the original Apollo astronauts nearly fifty years ago. It's priceless."

She set the vial back down in the aluminum suitcase and carefully peeled her gloves off, one by one. Then she reached up and grasped the plastic arm of her sunglasses, slowly lowering them down to the bridge of her nose. Her green eyes pierced Charlie as if they were searing right through his head.

"A significant amount of these moon rocks went missing from NASA's vaults a few months ago. We were close to finding them; then our lead fizzled out."

She handed Charlie one of the white gloves and signaled with a nod for him to put it on. As he pulled the soft material over his fingers, he could feel the remnant warmth from Anastasia's skin. When the glove was fully covering his skin, Anastasia pointed to the vial in the suitcase.

Charlie stared at her. She nodded again, and Charlie gingerly reached for the vial. It felt light—almost too light—in his hand. He held the glass close to his eyes, looking at the rock inside.

"We need your help, Charlie. I can explain everything—but not here. If you're willing to hear more, meet us at the Museum of Science today, after school. And I will tell you the rest."

Charlie looked at the rock for a moment more, then carefully placed the vial back into the foam padding in the center of the briefcase. It had felt good to hold something so incredibly rare—not because of how much it might be worth, but because he knew how lucky he was just to have even seen a piece of the moon. He thought back to the documentary he had watched with his father, which showed the phenomenal effort it had taken to get that first rocket into space, that first man all the way to that first, giant leap. Thousands of the greatest scientific minds in history had worked together to make it possible. The Apollo astronauts who had brought those moon rocks back to Earth were real and true heroes.

The woman in front of him—with her sunglasses;

her marble, silent partner; and her steel suitcase—was more of a mystery. But a chance to work for NASA, no matter how bizarre it sounded—well, that was something Charlie couldn't easily pass up.

At the very least, he owed it to those hero astronauts to hear what this woman had to say.

4

A CONTINUOUS BAND OF rubber with a single twist, rotating over a chain of metal cogs. Twisting and turning behind a pane of bulletproof glass, so close Charlie could hear the whir of the mechanics, could smell the grease that kept the cogs forever spinning. No matter how many times Charlie had stood in that exact place, staring through that viewing panel—dull and scratched in the center from so many years of wear and tear—it never got old. A masterpiece of physics and engineering, and yet in this place barely an exhibit, just a little detail that most visitors walked right past.

"It's just an escalator," Jeremy said, spindly arms crossed as he stood next to Charlie by the window. "I mean, the inside of an escalator. You're the only kid

I know who can get so excited by a darn escalator."

Jeremy was right; on the surface, it was just an escalator. More accurately, the revealed inside of the escalator that ran up the spine of Boston's Museum of Science,
one of the premier science museums in the entire country. Charlie had been to the museum many times with
his parents and friends; as a toddler, he had spent nearly
every Saturday morning racing from exhibit to exhibit,
his father huffing and puffing to keep up. Located on
a beautiful twist of the Charles River, with a view of
the duck boats purring along the banks of the neck-
lace of parks that connected Back Bay with the interior
of the city and Beacon Hill, the museum was beloved
by science-minded kids within a hundred-mile radius.
Here, even an escalator could be something to marvel
at, from the inside out.

"On top it's an escalator. Inside, it's a Möbius strip.
A band of rubber that can rotate round and round, pulling the steps up forever—and because of the Möbius
motion, no side of the band ever gets worn out."

Jeremy sighed. He'd been to the museum with
Charlie before, maybe hundreds of times. They'd grown
up together—heck, their parents had met in childbirth
classes months before either of them were born.

"So you brought me here to look at the escalator

again? I turned down a trip to the circus with my annoying little sister for this?"

Charlie blinked hard, finally pulling himself away from the glass viewing panel. He felt a little bad about the circus. Jeremy's parents had invited Charlie along too, and it had been tricky to explain to both sets of parents that they'd rather spend their afternoon at the Museum of Science. Charlie had considered telling his own dad the truth—the woman, Anastasia, had been Charlie's dad's student, after all—but he wanted to know more, first, and in his mind, information held back wasn't really lying, was it?

No matter how interesting or hypnotic the inside of an escalator was, watching the Möbius strip wasn't why they were really there. They were on a mission.

Charlie took Jeremy by the hand and pulled him around the corner to the base of the escalator. They stepped on in unison and began the slow descent to the museum's bottom floor.

"Jeremy, just follow my lead."

"You're really not going to tell me why we're here?"

Charlie paused a beat. Then he shrugged.

"The truth is, I'm not really sure. The woman, Anastasia, just told me to meet her here. And I didn't want to go alone. So—"

"So you dragged me here even though they think you are coming alone? I don't know, Charlie. I don't have a good feeling about this. I don't want to get into any trouble. My parents are still trying to figure out if they should be punishing me for what we did at Incredo Land or getting me some sort of trophy."

"These people have *moon rocks*," Charlie said. "The real thing. They aren't doing anything illegal. Trust me. They know my dad. They're NASA."

Charlie had uttered the magic word. Jeremy's eyes turned to saucers. NASA was a sort of Holy Grail to the Whiz Kids, maybe even better than Harvard or MIT.

Jeremy didn't say anything after that, but Charlie was certain he was interested enough to trust Charlie for the rest of the afternoon. The escalator steps creaked as they were whisked downward into the underbelly of the museum. They stepped out onto a dingy, gray, utilitarian rug spanning the entirety of the huge room. To the right, the blue wing had an open ceiling and courtyard-style architecture. The minor bits of wall space that were not covered with displays bore an eighties-era, lime-green paint job. The place was bustling with the after-school crowd, maybe a hundred kids of various ages bouncing about in groups as large as ten, but because of the open-courtyard format, it didn't feel crowded. It was just after four p.m., and Charlie could see that groups of kids were already gathering in the workshop area, a cordoned-off section of the atrium with striped carpeting, beneath a huge yellow sign that read ENGINEERING DESIGN WORKSHOP.

The only adults nearby were the museum volunteers, garbed in red lab coats: two standing behind the main engineering booth, two standing at the testing table, and a fifth standing next to a huge, vertical, Plexiglas tube. As Charlie and Jeremy got nearer, Charlie could hear the whir of a fan blowing air up through the clear cylindrical structure. The tube had to be at least nine feet tall, almost reaching the yellow sign. At the moment, one of the volunteers by the testing table was putting the finishing touches on what appeared to be a paper airplane; after a few final folds, he took the airplane and placed it into an opening at the bottom of the Plexiglas tube. Immediately, the plane leaped upward, buoyed on a blast of air from the fan. It rose halfway up the tube, settling between a pair of red lines, then spun around once, and slowly dropped back down.

Pretty cool. Charlie had been to many engineering workshops at the museum before; a sort of competition, the goal was always to apply some sort of engineering principle, to design some type of object—be it a plane, a boat, a car, etc.—that, on a miniature scale, worked the way a larger version of the object was supposed to work. Today's project looked to be to make a paper airplane that was folded perfectly enough to rise to the two red lines in the tube. As simple as that seemed, Charlie knew it actually involved some really advanced physics. Aeronautics comprised so many complicated principles—lift, thrust, torque—that to someone like Charlie, folding a paper airplane could never just be *folding a paper airplane.*

"Hey," Jeremy whispered, as they took a few more steps toward the testing table. "Looks like your friends got here first."

Charlie followed Jeremy's gaze. Anastasia and her stone colleague stood out like sore thumbs. They were still in their dark suits, and the woman also hadn't removed those ridiculous sunglasses. Too well dressed to be parents, too old and serious-looking to be museum volunteers.

"Let me do the talking," Charlie reminded Jeremy.

He was pretty sure the invitation from Anastasia had been for him alone; but he hadn't felt right not at least including his best friend. He had kept Jeremy in the dark once before—when he'd brought Jeremy along to Incredo Land to beat the amusement park, without letting Jeremy know what he'd really been up to—and it hadn't felt good at all. He'd sworn not to deceive any of the Whiz Kids ever again; they were a team—they always had each other's backs. So if Charlie was going to get himself into another adventure, this time he wasn't heading into the mist alone.

"Anastasia, Mr. Porter. I want you to meet my friend, Jeremy Draper. I know he doesn't look like much, but he's a master physicist. Sometimes even better than me."

Charlie could feel Jeremy tugging at his sleeve. Jeremy was good at physics, sure, but nobody had ever called him a *master* before. And certainly, he wasn't in Charlie's *league*.

Anastasia turned those sunglasses toward Jeremy. Jeremy seemed to shrink a few inches as she inspected him up and down. The stone man, Porter, didn't shift his gaze from Charlie. He just kept on staring with those cold blue eyes.

Before Anastasia could respond, Charlie reached for one of the sheets of paper from the testing table and passed it to Jeremy.

"He's really a genius," Charlie said. "He even won a junior Noble Prize for his work on aerodynamics, back in fifth grade."

"A *Nagassack* Noble Prize," Jeremy piped in,

fumbling with the sheet of paper, his long fingers nearly tying themselves in knots as he tried to make a semblance of a paper airplane. The prize had been Nagassack's version of the Nobel Prize, and was the highest honor in the school's science department. One was awarded each year to a student who was voted for by all of the teachers to have achieved some sort of advancement in science, be it an experiment, a presentation, or an invention. The boundaries were limitless, but the prize was only one. When questioned about the spelling of the prize by the principal, the science teachers told him that they thought it was a cool play on words to change the name to "noble" despite the renowned prize being named after Swedish inventor Alfred Nobel, because the winner of this prize at Nagassack was indeed considered "noble" for his or her achievement.

"Nonetheless, Jeremy, you won the prize. You're like . . . an Einstein of flight—"

"Okay, okay," Anastasia finally exhaled. "He can stay. And yes, as I think you've begun to guess, the science of flight—aerodynamics—is at the core of why we've come to you. More specifically, well, this."

She waved her hand toward the entire engineering design area, where kids had now begun folding paper airplanes on either side of them. Charlie raised an eyebrow.

"Paper airplanes? I thought you said rocket propulsion. . . ."

"Rocket propulsion and paper airplanes have a lot more to do with one another than you might realize. Yes, it was your paper on rocket propulsion that got us interested in you in the first place. But what we need from you—I guess, what we need from both of you—has to do with paper airplanes. Charlie, Jeremy, to be blunt: We need you to use your scientific abilities to infiltrate a paper airplane–building contest."

Charlie stared at her. *What does she mean by "infiltrate"?* Jeremy was halfway into folding his airplane, and it looked like something a four-year-old might make: stubby at the front, too wide at the back. As Charlie stood there, churning what Anastasia had just said in his mind, one of the volunteers handed him his own piece of blank paper. He began to fold it, starting with a crease right down the middle.

"A paper airplane–building contest?" he asked, as his fingers worked the paper.

"In Washington, DC. It's a week-long competition, involving twenty teams of kids. It's a distance competition; two members from a team of up to five compete to see who can make a plane that goes the farthest. But the rules are tough. Paper only, no tape, no other materials. And the kids who compete are good. Really good. This won't be a Nagassack Noble Prize. The other teams come from all over the country. This will be on a national level."

She continued to explain the rules: Each team would have three minutes to design, fold, and prepare a paper airplane out of an 8.5-by-11-inch piece of standard twenty-pound copy paper. The team would consist of up to five members, but only two could do the actual physical competition: One would act as the folder, the other the thrower. The three nonparticipating contributors could provide verbal support during the competition but would not be allowed to touch the paper. The design of the plane could change, but that's where experience and expertise came in. You could alter your design or go with a previous design, and designs did not need to be original. Because it would be a live competition, the feat of folding the plane was part of the competition, so repeated designs were allowed.

Charlie waved his half-built paper airplane at the two suits.

"Why do you need us?"

Anastasia lowered her voice.

"The team that has won for the past three years is led by a kid genius named Richard Caldwell. He was groomed as a newbie fourth grader three years ago and today is the reigning captain. Maybe you've heard that name before. He's the son of a former astronaut, Buzz Caldwell, who now runs a private rocket-building company, Aerospace Infinity. We need someone who can fit right in seamlessly with Richard and the other teams. Someone with a science background who understands thrust, acceleration, and the physics involved in flight. But understanding all of those concepts is not all that's required. Stamina, motivation, and a drive to succeed are all necessary qualities to make it to the end of the competition. We don't expect you to be a champion, but we do need you to at least get into the finals."

Charlie had certainly heard of Buzz Caldwell—heck, he had a poster of the man on the door to his closet. One of the original space shuttle astronauts, Caldwell had been to space six times. He'd never been to the moon, of course—nobody had been to the moon since the Apollo program ended in the early seventies—but he'd been in orbit, again and again. He was a true American hero.

Charlie didn't know anything about his son, Richard—but being the kid of a real live astronaut must have been incredible. No surprise the kid was a genius.

"The competition takes place at the Smithsonian's Air and Space Museum, but is partially sponsored by Caldwell's company," Anastasia said. "We want you to enter the competition and get to the finals because we believe Aerospace Infinity is somehow involved with the missing moon rocks. We have reason to believe that the rocks are inside their labs somewhere—but we can't investigate as we normally would, because Caldwell is a national hero. We can't accuse an astronaut of being involved in stolen moon rocks unless we have solid evidence. And that's where you come in. You could help us get that evidence—if you can get inside Aerospace Infinity."

Charlie took a deep breath. So they wanted him to get inside this aerospace company by getting to the finals of a paper airplane competition. It sounded exciting, but the idea of going after one of the original space shuttle astronauts gave Charlie chills.

"How can Buzz Caldwell be involved with stealing moon rocks? I can't believe he'd do anything like that."

"That's what we need to find out. Maybe it's someone who works under him. Maybe it's all some sort of big mistake. All we know is that witnesses have seen those moon rocks within the Aerospace Infinity labs.

We're not sure where those labs are, but we need someone to get inside, to investigate. Charlie, think of it this way: You could clear Buzz Caldwell's name. And you don't have to worry—I've just spoken to your father, right before you arrived here. I told him all about the paper airplane competition. He's given his permission for the trip to DC."

"You told him about the moon rocks?" Charlie asked. Charlie hadn't seen his dad since he'd left for school that morning. Jeremy's parents had dropped them off at the museum, instead of the circus. "And about Buzz?"

"Not exactly. The moon rocks and an American astronaut's involvement are a matter of national security. These things are strictly confidential. Charlie, Jeremy, you need to keep these things secret. NASA is counting on you."

Charlie felt his heart pounding. Of course his parents would approve of him entering a science competition. But would they really approve of him doing something that was so secretive? Then again—it was NASA.

"And just so you know," Anastasia added, "the competition winners get a special invitation to visit NASA with their families, and a cash prize of thirty thousand dollars for each student. And if you help us with the moon rocks, I can promise you that your names will reach the highest levels at our organization. One day, you could be working right alongside us."

Charlie looked at Jeremy and could see the excitement in his friend's eyes. Then Charlie glanced down at the paper in his hands. Two more folds, and it looked kind of like an airplane. He nodded at Jeremy, and they both grabbed their respective planes and headed to the Plexiglas airflow tube. One by one, they handed their creations to the volunteer working the testing area. The volunteer's red braids were almost the same color as her coat, and her pale skin was as white as the paper being used for the planes. She took the two planes and opened the hatch in the lower part of the tube.

"What did you name your planes?" the volunteer asked.

Charlie thought for a moment.

"Mine's named *Moon Rock*."

Jeremy laughed.

"Mine's *NNPF*, short for *Nagassack Noble Prize Fighter*!" he said a little too loudly.

The volunteer shrugged, then placed the two planes into the tube.

In one swift whir of the fan, both planes rose up a few inches—then plummeted straight back down, crashing into the fan at the base of the tube. There was a loud metallic groan as the fan chopped the planes to pieces. Then a cough as it spat them both back out, right up the tube and out the top—minced into a plume of snowy paper confetti.

Charlie blushed as he glanced back toward Anastasia and her partner. Anastasia was looking away, equally embarrassed by the display. But Porter was staring directly at Charlie, his eyes narrowed to snakelike slits.

NASA, Charlie reminded himself. *Astronauts and moon rocks.*

Watching the paper confetti raining down around him, he had to admit that maybe he didn't know as much about the physics of flight as he'd thought. But if there was one thing Charlie knew about himself for sure—he was a fast learner. They didn't call him Numbers for nothing.

5

IT WAS WELL AFTER five by the time Jeremy's parents dropped Charlie off at the end of his driveway, but even so, he took his time marching the last few yards to his front door. The white slats running up above the door to the roof of his house needed a fresh coat of paint, worn down from the past few New England winters. His home was typical for the area. Newton was known for its cookie-cutter homes, near enough to each other to foster a nice neighborhood feel, but far enough so that if you wanted privacy, you only needed to erect a white picket fence. Charlie's dad had never quite gotten to the fence, but still they barely knew their neighbors. That's what happened when you had two professors for parents, who had always been

more comfortable with their heads in scientific jour-
nals than gathering in the yards of neighbors for block
parties and barbecues.

Par for the course, Charlie could see his dad sitting
on the couch in the living room, reading an old issue of
Nature, as he entered the front door. From the kitchen
on the other side of the living room, Charlie could smell
the distinct odor of burnt toast. Since his mom taught
evening classes most weekdays, Charlie's dad had taken
to making dinner for the two of them, and burnt grilled
cheese was usually somewhere on their Spartan menu.

"Let me guess, Dad. Grilled cheese?"

His dad looked up from the magazine, and it took a
full beat for the nerdy glaze to fade enough for him to
recognize his own kid. Then he offered a wide smile.

"You got it, Charles!"

Charlie dropped onto the couch next to his dad. He
decided to get right into things; if he waited too long,
his dad would be back into the magazine, and Charlie
would lose his chance. Grilled cheese, bath, bedtime.
Somewhere in that timeline his mom would wander
home, maybe turn on some classical music, and then
she and Charlie's dad would be off on some deep, scientific debate until well after Charlie was fast asleep.

"Dad," Charlie said, as his father eagerly eyed the

magazine. "I met some pretty cool people today, and they say they know you."

His dad thought for a moment, then finally remembered.

"Anastasia Federov. That's right, she called me this afternoon. So nice to hear from her. A quiet student, if I remember, but she had a lot of promise. Some real engineering skills. Shame that she let it go to waste."

"What do you mean?" Charlie asked. The woman worked at NASA, after all. That didn't sound like a waste to him.

"Well, from what I'd heard through the grapevine, she'd dropped out of grad school shortly after she took my class. Never finished her degree. I hadn't heard from her since, until today."

"But she's still involved with NASA."

"It seems so," Charlie's dad said. "She told me she wanted to sponsor you in some sort of competition. Aeronautics, was it?"

"So you know about the competition? She said you'd given your permission. What did Mom say?"

Charlie and his dad had a habit of keeping little secrets from Charlie's mom—nothing serious, but they liked to think some things were "need to know." Like, for instance, when Charlie had mistakenly blown up one of his mom's vases with a homemade firecracker. Or frozen the paint off the bathroom wall during a liquid nitrogen experiment that his dad was supposedly supervising.

"I haven't had a chance to tell her yet. But I wanted to wait until you decided whether or not you were going to do it. DC isn't that far, but a week on your own is still a pretty big deal."

Charlie wouldn't be on his *own*, of course. The Whiz Kids would be with him. At first, he'd thought it would just be Jeremy; but after his display with the airplanes at the Museum of Science, Anastasia had agreed to let him choose a team to help him. It had been easy to come up with three perfect names to add to his roster.

"I don't know, Dad. I want to enter the competition, but there's more to the game than just paper airplanes."

Charlie's dad fingered the *Nature* magazine, then ran a hand through Charlie's mop of brown hair.

"Son, I know you get worked up when it comes to things like this. I know you don't take competition lightly, and you always try harder than might be necessary. But you have to remember: It isn't about winning. Sometimes we're even prouder of you when you lose."

Charlie wanted to explain to his dad that this time, it wasn't about winning or losing at all; it was about stolen moon rocks. For a brief second, he considered telling his dad everything; but he knew that would probably lead to a phone call to Anastasia, and then Charlie would have broken her trust right from the start. He'd be able to forget NASA, the $30,000 cash prize, the trip to DC. *A matter of national security*, she'd said. It sounded a little overly dramatic, but then again, anything involving Buzz Caldwell was likely to be dramatic.

"How can you be proud even when I lose?" Charlie finally said. His dad grinned.

"Well, sometimes you actually *win* by losing."

He turned back to his magazine, and for a moment Charlie thought the conversation was over, that his dad would be lost in whatever scientific article had caught his attention for the evening. But to his surprise, his dad reached down and carefully tore one of the pages out of the magazine, then handed the shiny sheet of paper to Charlie.

"Let's see what you got, kid."

Charlie took a deep breath, then carefully started manipulating the page. He made a crease down the center. Then smoothed the two sides, folding two corners at an angle. His goal was to keep it simple. Nothing fancy. At the very least, he didn't want a repeat of what had happened at the museum.

He pulled the outer corners down again and made a sharp point, then folded the wings outward, carefully matching the sides. This was it. This was going to be the best plane ever.

Charlie and his father carefully looked over the folded plane. Then, without a word, Charlie cocked his elbow back and tossed the plane into the air, hoping to see it soar across the living room.

For the first few feet, everything seemed to be going perfectly. The plane tore through the air, rising high toward the ceiling. And then, suddenly, it jerked up— then took a quick nosedive straight down, slamming into the hardwood floor.

"Three feet," Charlie's dad laughed. "A new world record."

Charlie grimaced. He and the Whiz Kids had a lot of work to do.

But his decision was made. He was heading to Washington, DC.

6

"LADIES AND GENTLEMEN, IN a few minutes we
will be reaching our top cruising speed of one hundred
fifty miles per hour. Sit tight, and enjoy the fastest train
in the continental US!"

Streaks of color zoomed by the rectangular window,
a few inches from Charlie's face, as he clutched at the
lightly padded armrests of his business class seat. Sure,
train travel didn't bother him as much as flying. Speed,
on its own, didn't scare him, and the rumble of the
tracks beneath the Acela's wheels was somewhat sooth-
ing, even though the way the rocket-shaped chassis
rocked back and forth as it took the soft turns, keeping
itself vaguely parallel to the Eastern Seaboard shoreline
outside the trembling window, was mildly unnerving.

But the Acela wasn't just a train; having been designed to resemble the French TGV, with 6,200-horsepower engines, the Acela was America's version of a bullet train, the fastest class of rail-based travel. Despite its international nickname—"the pig," so called because of the heavy weight requirements of the US Federal Railroad Administration—the Acela managed to reach its top speed of over 150 miles per hour in two stretches between Boston and New York. They'd just entered the first stretch, and it was as thrilling, and terrifying, as Charlie had expected.

"Kentaro, hold on tight!" yelled Jeremy from across the aisle. "You're liable to blow right out the window!"

The train vibrated even harder as Kentaro clutched his bright neon backpack to his chest, scrunching up his face and sticking out his tongue in response to Jeremy's harassment. That ridiculous backpack had been a hot topic of conversation for the Whiz Kids ever since their parents had put them on the train, back at South Station in Boston. Jeremy was the last of the five to sit down and ended up in a four seater alone directly across from his teammates. But the short thirty inches across the train aisle didn't stop him from torturing Kentaro. The backpack was bright orange, with neon-yellow shapes inked all over the fabric in a graffiti-like pattern. Just like most things that Kentaro had brought back from his family's yearly visit to Japan, it was small in size but huge in visual impact. To the Whiz Kids, it looked like it had been designed for a toddler, but it fit Kentaro's body perfectly.

Kentaro tilted his head toward the window, now fully engrossed in the speed-blurred panorama outside. From Charlie's angle, he really did look like a little kid; Kentaro was sitting next to Crystal, and his head barely cleared the top of her chin. But despite his tiny size, he was the language powerhouse of the Whiz Kids. Having been reading in five different languages since kindergarten, he'd made winning two state spelling bees in consecutive years seem like a piece of cake. At age six, he had been deemed too small for peewee soccer, so instead of kicking a ball, he'd found himself moving tiles around on a Scrabble board, and had placed second in a regional high school tournament.

Sitting directly across from Kentaro in the fourth seat, next to Charlie, was Marion Tuttle. He looked up from his sketch pad for a split second—not to defend Kentaro against Jeremy's jibes, but because Anastasia and Porter walked by with a couple of cardboard-box trays full of food. Realizing it would be a while before they got to them, he ducked his head back down and kept drawing. He was truly the artist of the group. When you needed anything drawn or images computer generated, Marion was your man. With his pudgy fingers you wouldn't think he could whip up the sort of designs that would impress art professors, but in mere minutes, he could produce something that looked like da Vinci had drawn it himself. His tool of choice was usually a simple Bic pen—nothing fancy, just a regular ballpoint, with a plastic cap that he liked to chew on while he worked.

As the train continued to roar past the Connecticut countryside, Marion bit down a few more times on the blue plastic, his freckled cheeks bouncing up and down with each chomp.

"Seems like you've got enough to eat," Crystal said, pointing to the gnarled pen cap. "Probably just as tasty as a bag of old, slightly warm nuts."

Marion barely glanced up from his drawing.

"According to my last visit to the Children's Hospital allergy wing, my blood levels are reading one hundred plus for peanuts. So nobody better go for the nuts. A little peanut dust blows my way, you're going to get a quick lesson on the proper use of an EpiPen."

Peanuts were just one of Marion's many food-related enemies: coconut, gluten, shellfish—heck, it was amazing how many foods he had to avoid on a daily basis, especially considering his robust build. And foods were just one of the many components of his allergic makeup; he'd actually once spent an entire week in a hospital because of an ant bite. The doctors at Children's were still writing papers on the episode a year later, trying to understand how a two-millimeter ant had caused a 110-pound sixth grader to have a nearly life-threatening reaction.

"Please, no EpiPens on this trip," Charlie begged. "And let's keep the fooling around to a minimum. I get the feeling our 'proctors' have a pretty low tolerance for monkey business."

Charlie glanced down four rows, to where Anastasia and Porter were sitting and presumably organizing the food trays. Anastasia's wide-brimmed hat was just visible over the vinyl of the seat back behind her. The stone man's square head, on the other hand, rose a good eight inches above the vinyl. His crew cut seemed to catch the light from the panels on the ceiling, each short strand glowing like threads of supercharged fiberglass.

"Yeah," Crystal whispered, leaning over the table. "About them. They give me the creeps. If there wasn't the possibility of actually getting to see and touch a moon rock, live and in person at the museum, I'd be back in fourth-period study hall right now."

Although Charlie had kept his silence with his father about the real reason they were on their way to DC for a paper airplane contest, he hadn't thought once about keeping anything from the rest of the Whiz Kids. He'd learned his lesson at Incredo Land; they were a team, in every sense of the word. If they were going to have a chance at winning this thing, there couldn't be any secrets between them.

"Sure," Jeremy said. "You'd much rather be dodging Dylan in the hallways than staying in a fancy hotel in Washington, DC, playing with paper airplanes, possibly winning enough money to afford college tuition for a year. Such a sacrifice you're making."

Crystal answered by sticking out her tongue. Jeremy was about to reach for it with his fingers when the train conductor came back over the intercom:

"Next stop, New Haven!"

As the train started to slow from the 150-mile-per-hour top speed, many of the adults in the seats around them rose, reaching for briefcases and carry-ons. Charlie had never been to New Haven, but he knew it was a fairly large city in Connecticut—part industrial town, part academic oasis, especially where the Ivy League school Yale was located. He watched as the train pulled into the concrete-covered station, and the business-people made their way to the doors.

After the passengers had disembarked, new passengers began piling in. Charlie saw a small group of kids clamber aboard, all carrying matching green backpacks. The packs were emblazoned with huge white letters: WORTH HOOKS MIDDLE SCHOOL. The kids looked to be about Charlie's age, and he began to wonder: *Are these kids part of the competition?*

Before he could voice his thoughts out loud, something flashed just above his line of sight. He looked up in time to see something white and pointy floating across the top of the cabin, a good foot above the tallest passenger's head. The rest of the Whiz Kids followed his gaze and watched together as the paper airplane flew the entire length of the train car.

"Holy cow," Jeremy said.

How could something so graceful and powerful be made by simple folds on a piece of paper? When the plane finally crashed into the far wall of the train, falling to the floor, Charlie turned his head back down the aisle and watched as the Worth Hooks kids, all five of them, filed in one after another, filling the empty seats just a row away from where the Whiz Kids were seated.

"Why don't you take a picture?" a freckled boy said as he lowered himself into a seat directly across the aisle. "It will last longer."

The kid was tall, maybe six inches taller than Charlie, and had thick arms. Every inch of him seemed covered in those patches of freckles.

"Sorry," Charlie said. "Didn't mean to stare. Heck of a paper plane. Did you make that?"

"What paper plane? I think your mind's playing tricks on you, kid. I don't see anything on this train but a herd of nerds."

A flowery scent filled Charlie's nostrils as a girl moved through the aisle and took the outer seat next to the freckled kid, pushing him toward the window.

"Don't mind Ryan. He was raised by cavemen. I'm Kelly. That's Jack, Michael, and Ross. Worth Hooks Middle School, outside New Haven. Are you guys from Boston?"

Charlie felt a familiar burst of awkwardness as he took in her long blond hair and rounded cheekbones.

He'd never been good talking to girls—other than Crystal—and girls like Kelly, well, they might as well have been aliens for all he knew how to communicate with them. But he knew that sitting there with his mouth open, staring, wasn't going to make a great first impression.

"Uh, yeah. Well, Newton, actually. Nagassack Middle. Where are you guys headed?"

"DC," Kelly responded. "And yes, that was one of our planes. We're going to a national paper plane contest. I'm guessing, since you're all about the right age—except maybe your friend with the Day-Glo backpack—you're on your way to the same place?"

The train had started up again, the car suddenly swaying side to side so aggressively that Charlie nearly fell into the aisle. Kelly was caught in the motion as well, and for a brief second their faces almost touched. Charlie pulled back in pure embarrassment, heaving himself a little too hard, nearly pinning Marion against the window.

"Geez, Casanova," Ryan shouted, "you work quick. Going in for a kiss before we're ten feet out of the station. You'll be picking out wedding chapels by the time we reach Washington."

Charlie turned bright red. He could see Crystal pursing her lips across the table from him, disgusted by his awkward display. Jeremy and Kentaro were trying to hold back laughter.

"Sorry," Charlie mumbled.

Kelly just smiled at him. "Hey, nothing to be sorry about. I like a confident competitor. If you're as good at making airplanes as you are at breaking the ice with girls, we're going to be in for quite a battle."

Charlie's face couldn't have gone any deeper red if he'd stuck it in a bucket of paint. He wanted to scream that he hadn't been going for a kiss. Heck, he'd never kissed a girl in his life, unless you counted his mom, and he wasn't planning on starting with a total stranger, in the middle of a crowded train, with everyone watching. But he had a feeling that opening his mouth was just going to embarrass him, and it already felt like his head was about to explode.

Instead, he just tried to smile back. Since Crystal chose that exact moment to kick him as hard as she could in his right shin, what he managed was much more of a scowl.

"Keep your mind on the game," Crystal whispered across the table. "We're not here to make friends. We're here to build airplanes."

Charlie knew she was right. The problem was, he was pretty sure the girl across the aisle was a heck of a lot better at both.

7

"OH MAN, THIS IS pretty posh. I think we might be underdressed."

Charlie followed Jeremy through huge wooden double doors, stopping dead at the edge of a vast ballroom. Although it was only a quarter past six and the welcome party was supposed to have begun a few minutes ago, the place was already packed, filled with well-coiffed sixth graders from one opulent wall to the other.

"I feel like we're in one of those scenes at the beginning of a Batman movie," Kentaro chimed in from somewhere to Charlie's left. "Any minute now, the Joker is going to come down from the ceiling and take everyone hostage."

"We should be so lucky," Crystal said.

Charlie smiled, but he could sense that she was only half kidding. Crystal put on a good front, but he knew she suffered from the same anxieties and shyness as the rest of them; being outsiders at an age when everyone did his or her best not to stand out from the crowd left little room for real confidence. And even a kid who was pretty sure of himself would have been sweating at the sight in front of them.

The Moretti Grand Ballroom of the Watergate Hotel would have been a daunting setting even if it wasn't filled with more than a hundred kids decked out in their Sunday best. The Watergate was actually one of five buildings in the historic complex built in the late sixties, named after the wooden water gate that controlled the flow of a man-made canal running perpendicular to the mighty Potomac River. When the hotel first opened in 1967, it had been considered a playground for the rich and powerful: champagne splashing across the pool deck, Hollywood stars mingling with Capitol Hill elite. On June 17, 1972, the hotel became famous for a different reason altogether: At around two in the morning, five men broke into suite 600, which at the time housed the Democratic National Committee's headquarters. When it turned out that at least two of the men were on President Richard Nixon's payroll, the infamous scandal led to the resignation of a sitting US president.

Charlie had never imagined that by midway through sixth grade, he'd be setting foot in a hotel famous enough to have changed history. As he stared across the crowded hall, with its fifteen-foot ceilings, original fixtures, and huge picture windows that looked out over the Potomac, it almost seemed like he was traveling back in time. The ballroom—named after celebrity architect Luigi Moretti, who had dared create a curved building at a time when most buildings were square—dripped gravitas, which meant that Charlie and his Whiz Kids stood out like five sore thumbs.

"Just remember why we're here," Charlie said. "We're here to win a contest."

Judging from the crowd, there was little chance of that happening anyway. To Charlie's left, he saw a kid ordering a Coke from a tuxedo-wearing bartender. The kid looked no older than eleven, with spiky brown hair, but he was wearing a full seersucker suit, like something right out of a black-and-white movie. Next to him, two other boys had on matching navy blazers, with plaid shirts and khaki pants. Beyond the boys sat a table of girls in black dresses, all of them with their hair pulled back in tight ponytails.

As for the Whiz Kids, the best dressed of their crew

had to be Crystal, who had managed to throw on a peach, faux-crystal-encrusted T-shirt dress. Charlie had on his favorite Batman long sleeve sweatshirt and faded jeans. Jeremy had a Spider-Man crewneck. Kentaro was wearing a neon jumpsuit, and Marion had on something gray and old, which looked suspiciously like his Nagassack PE uniform.

"Well, since we made it this far, we may as well eat," Marion said, immediately splitting off toward the buffet table that ran along one of the ballroom's curved walls. "I think I see mini-burgers. You think they have gluten-free buns? Hopefully one of these penguins in their tuxes has an ingredients list."

Kentaro and Jeremy gave Charlie a look, then followed Marion toward the steaming chrome trays. Charlie was about to join them when Crystal touched his arm.

"We shouldn't waste any time. If we're going to find Richard Caldwell in this crowd, we'll have to work together."

She was right, of course. Anastasia had passed Charlie a photograph of Caldwell on their way off the train at Washington's Union Station, and though they'd had plenty of time to study the picture during the cab ride to the hotel, it was going to be tricky to pick him out from a distance. Auburn hair, longish in the front, with blue eyes and a good, square jaw. His dad might have been a famous astronaut, but Caldwell looked exactly like a million other prep-school middle schoolers.

Even so, Charlie was hoping to find their target as early in the night as he could. Despite what he'd just told the Whiz Kids, winning the paper airplane contest wasn't their mission—they were there to get close to Caldwell. If Caldwell really was the genius Anastasia had said he was, then getting to the finals of the contest would be the best way to ensure they got to know one another. But if Charlie could lay some groundwork, even from the beginning, it might make things easier down the line.

He led Crystal a few yards deeper into the mob, pushing between boys in fitted suits and girls in long, elegant dresses. He scanned the nearest round tables, where some of the teams had set up shop, their ceramic plates piled high with fancy hors d'oeuvres, amid towers of gleaming silverware. Charlie doubted Marion was going to find mini-hamburgers in any of the chrome trays on the buffet line. Or any gluten-free buns for that matter. Heck, Charlie doubted Marion would be able to pronounce any of the items the other kids were eating, let alone digest them.

He passed another pair of round tables, then pushed across a tightly packed carpeted section at the center of the room, directly beneath a huge Swarovski chandelier. From below, the chandelier looked a little like a sleeping octopus—each shiny tentacle swaying with the classical music being pumped into the room from hidden speakers above the giant windows. Then they were past the edge of the carpet, heading beyond a small stage set between a pair of potted trees. There was a podium on the stage, and on the podium, a large golden trophy, shaped like a 1920s airplane. Propeller in front, long stiff wings hanging out from each side, a pair of wheels beneath a bullet-shaped cockpit, and a tail that seemed a little too long for its body. The plane looked vaguely familiar, but Charlie couldn't quite place it. He was about to ask Crystal what it was, when a blond ponytail swung right past his head, nearly hitting him in the nose. The trophy airplane might have been familiar, but the floral scent that hit him full in the face was unforgettable.

"Thought that was you," Kelly said, spinning to a stop directly in front of Charlie and Crystal, her back to the stage and the podium. "Admiring the trophy? It's going to look a lot cooler when I'm up there accepting it for my team—from a real live astronaut."

She grinned, adjusting her green backpack over one shoulder. Aside from the backpack, she had cleaned up nicely; her dress was gray and ran all the way down past her knees. It was a strange thing indeed to see her toting her bag around a fancy party, but it wasn't the weirdest thing he had seen. Kentaro seemed to have the same sort of affinity to his own neon sack.

"An astronaut?" Charlie said, because he couldn't think of anything better. He wanted to tell this girl he barely knew that she looked great in gray, but there was no chance anything remotely close to that was going to come out of his mouth.

"Buzz Caldwell," Kelly nodded. "His kid is in the competition, and his company is a lead sponsor, so it's no surprise that they are hosting the winner's ceremony at the end of the week. I'm almost as excited about meeting an astronaut as I am about winning that prize money."

"Money isn't everything," Charlie tried, and Crystal made a sound to his left. She didn't seem to be enjoying his efforts at making conversation; or maybe she was just trying to stick to their agenda. Crystal didn't care much for *deviation*.

"I completely agree, but sometimes it's hard to think that way," Kelly said. "I think a lot of these kids are here for the trophy. But for some of us, the cash prize might be the only way we'll get to go to college at all."

Charlie felt like he'd just put his foot squarely in his mouth. Maybe it was the matching backpacks, but he had assumed Kelly was from a similar background as his. He knew he was privileged to have parents who were professors and to go to a school like Nagassack. His family wasn't rich, not by a long shot, but he was lucky to have other things to worry about than how he was going to go to college. ·

"Have you met him?" Crystal broke in, thankfully changing the subject before Charlie had a chance to say something stupid. "Not the astronaut—his son; I think his name is Richard? I hear he's some sort of genius."

"He's *every* sort of genius," Kelly said. "He's won this competition three years in a row. The first year, he was even officially too young to enter; they waived him in when one of his team members got sick the day before the competition started. I met him last year when we made the semifinals. His team killed us, but he was very nice about it—even gave me some pointers on how to extend my wing length to deal with the humidity factor."

Wing length. Humidity. Charlie glanced at Crystal, who had the same expression on her face. These were things they were supposed to understand. This wasn't going to be just folding a piece of paper a few times. There was real science behind this, and they were going to need to move fast to catch up to people like Kelly and Caldwell.

"I'd be happy to show you what he showed me," Kelly started, slinging her backpack in front of her so she could reach the zipper. "I always carry a stack of regulation paper with me, in case I get the urge to practice."

Charlie was surprised by Kelly's willingness to share such information. If she really needed the prize money to afford college, then why was she so willing to share? But he wasn't going to turn down valuable insight. Just as Kelly started reaching to open her bag, she was interrupted mid-zipper by a sudden, high-pitched wail that seemed to be coming from above the chandelier. Charlie swung around and saw flashing lights erupt across the ceiling.

"I think it's the fire alarm!" Crystal shouted.

Charlie's eyes widened. He didn't smell any smoke or see anything bright or orange—but the crowd began pushing back toward the way they'd come in. A hundred kids looked like a thousand when they were all moving at once. He searched the room for the other

Whiz Kids, but all he could see were strangers shoving and bumping their way toward the open double doors. He scanned along the walls and was surprised to see Kelly's teammate—the big red-headed kid named Ryan—standing right by an open, red-and-white fire alarm. He had a telling smirk on his face. The same smug look Charlie had seen many a time on Dylan Wigglesworth's face after he had done one of his myriad of pranks. It quickly became obvious to Charlie that Ryan had pulled the alarm for attention.

"I don't think it's a real fire," Charlie said, and both Kelly and Crystal matched his gaze.

Kelly exhaled. "I'm sorry about this. He's really not as bad as he seems. He's just got some, well, issues."

"He's got issues?" Crystal exclaimed. "He's a psycho. Pulling a fire alarm in a crowded ballroom?"

"Either way," Charlie said, "I think we should get out of here."

He saw Ryan slipping out through a fire exit and started in the same direction. Before he realized what was happening, Kelly had grabbed his hand and was heading through the crowd after him. He could hear Crystal grumbling from behind, "Wait up, guys." But he was being buffeted by the crowd now, barely keeping his footing. Still, he could feel Kelly's warm palm against his. Sparks moved up his arm, into his spine. He wasn't quite sure why, but this girl seemed to like him. And even though she was supposed to be his competition, even though she was basically a stranger, a teammate to the kind of kid who pulled fire alarms during reception banquets, he was starting to really like her, too.

It took a good five minutes, but soon Charlie found himself outside, standing on a curb near the back of the hotel, next to an alley filled with huge green garbage bins. Kelly was still holding his hand, and together they fought to catch their breath, as more kids streamed past them into the street. They could still hear the fire alarm blaring from the hall, mingling with the sound of sirens in the distance. The fire trucks would arrive soon, something Charlie would usually find exciting. But he couldn't think about much more than the strange fingers touching his.

"Now, that's chivalry." He heard Crystal's exasperated voice from the darkness to his left. "Leave me there to burst into flames as you two run off on a date."

Charlie could feel his face flushing. He wasn't sure why he felt a closeness to a girl he barely knew. Heck, he'd known Crystal for years, and it was like she was basically a sister to him. He quickly let Kelly's hand drop and feigned a cool-kid stance as he saw his friend stepping onto the curb next to him, her eyes angry behind her thick glasses.

"It wasn't a real fire."

Crystal was about to respond when Marion, Kentaro, and Jeremy crashed through the fire door together, almost jamming themselves in the door frame by trying to exit at the exact same time. Marion was breathing hard as he reached the curb. Jeremy looked terrified next to him, his red hair sticking up from his head in a demented halo. But Kentaro seemed perfectly calm; in fact, he was still shoving what looked to be a handful of jumbo shrimp into his mouth from an overloaded plate he was balancing in one hand.

"Are you crazy?" Marion screamed at him between breaths. "You could have gotten us killed, dillydallying around the buffet while the place burned down around us!"

"It wasn't a real fire. I saw that Ryan kid pull the alarm—"

"Yeah, me too. But did you ever think that maybe he pulled the alarm because he saw a fire?"

Kentaro thought for a moment. Then he shrugged.

"Still didn't seem like a good reason to waste some perfectly good shrimp."

Marion looked at Charlie and Crystal, then saw

Kelly standing there. Kelly pointed down the street: Virginia Avenue, which bisected the National Mall, heading toward the center of the capital city.

"Maybe we should all take a walk. I don't think the dinner will be starting up any time soon, and we may as well see the sights. DC is even cooler at night," said Kelly.

Charlie could tell that Crystal would have preferred to head back to their hotel rooms so they could get to work on their paper airplanes, but the rest of the Whiz Kids seemed game.

As for Charlie, he would have followed Kelly right back into the ballroom, even if it really was on fire.

8

THE TAILLIGHTS SPARKLED LIKE strings of Christmas lights, lying next to one another along the packed avenue to his right, as Charlie followed Kelly down the double-wide sidewalk, his Whiz Kids a few steps behind. The city was bustling and alive. At times they had to push their way through groups of tourists and gaggles of government workers, a surging tide of men and women wearing dresses and ties, moving faster than necessary in every direction at once. The sky had gone dark, but the sidewalks and streets were lit by orange streetlamps and the traffic itself, a never-ending snake of taxicabs, delivery vans, SUVs, and sleek limousines.

Walking next to Kelly, with his friends behind him, Charlie had never felt so free. He doubted his parents would have been thrilled with the idea of him wandering around a city as big as Washington, DC, without adult guidance, but Kelly didn't seem to have any reservations about a group of twelve-year-olds hitting the streets on their own. As she told Charlie more about her school and her upbringing, her street-smart attitude wasn't surprising: Worth Hooks wasn't exactly on the wrong side of the tracks, but most of the kids came from working-class families, a good portion even on some sort of public aid. Kelly's father worked in construction; her mother waited tables. She had an older brother who was about to graduate from high school—which was why she was keenly aware of what an opportunity winning the cash prize would be, what it would mean for her future. Her brother would be going to a local community college because that was what her parents could afford, and he'd be working part time to pay for his books and other expenses.

"Hey, I'm not complaining," she added. "A lot of kids have it way worse. That's why I can never get too upset when Ryan does something stupid—well, he's pretty much always doing something stupid. He hasn't had an easy time of it, growing up the way he has."

Charlie was so engrossed in her words, he almost didn't notice as they moved off the sidewalk and into the shadow of what could only be described as a massive marble temple. It was only when Kelly paused and pointed that he realized where they were standing.

"See, it's not really a fair race," Kelly finally continued, as they skirted the Lincoln Memorial and across the stone steps leading down to a flat expanse of paved stone, which separated Lincoln's perch from the Reflecting Pool. The towering, needlelike Washington Monument was now visible in the distance. "We don't all start at the same place when it comes to throwing the planes. I started pretty far back, but Ryan couldn't even see the starting line."

By the time they reached the edge of the vast, rectangular pool, Charlie had a better idea of what kind of a kid pulled a fire alarm during a welcome banquet. According to Kelly, Ryan's parents had gotten divorced when he was just a baby, and his father had skipped town by the time he was two. His two older brothers had dropped out of high school just before they'd been kicked out for fighting. But that was the least of Ryan's mom's concerns. The brothers also had pending charges of petty theft, among other delinquent charges. It wasn't a surprise that Ryan had basically raised himself. It didn't excuse his bad behavior, but it made it more understandable.

Standing at the edge of the long pool, staring across the glassy surface of the water, Charlie felt thankful for the things he had, and also for the nonquantifiable things like friendships, which were easy to take for granted. As Crystal, Jeremy, Marion, and Kentaro caught up, sidling next to him at the pool, he wondered what his life would have been like if he hadn't found friends like them. Probably pretty lonely. Being smart was a gift, but it wasn't everything—and it wasn't always enough.

Crystal pointed toward the giant Washington Monument, all the way on the other side of the pool, rising up into the darkness, as far as the eye could see.

"See how the monument is reflected across the water. The lights on each side of the pool make it into a natural mirror—"

She paused, midsentence, and Charlie noticed that she was suddenly squinting her eyes. He followed her gaze and saw that something was moving above the surface of the glassy water. Something white and sleek, moving fast, slicing the air about fifteen feet above the pool.

"What the heck is that?" Kentaro asked. "Is that a bird?"

Charlie shook his head. The object was gliding in a straight line, cutting through the air with a precision that seemed too perfect, too deliberate. For a brief second it seemed to rise a foot higher, catching a puff of wind running horizontally across the Mall, but then it continued toward them, seeming to gain speed. It wasn't until the object was a bare dozen feet away that Charlie realized what they were staring at.

A paper airplane.

"Is that what I think it is?" Crystal whispered.

The airplane sped the last yard to the end of the pool, then floated right past them, finally skidding down to the paved path just a half dozen feet to their left. Before Charlie or any of the others could move, a shape appeared out of the darkness along the side of the reflecting pool. It was a kid, about Charlie's age and height, jogging toward the now-landed paper plane. Even from that distance, in the soft light from around the pool, Charlie recognized that auburn hair, a little bit longer in the front.

"Richard Caldwell," Charlie whispered. Kelly nodded.

"In the flesh. Man, that plane cleared half the length of the Reflecting Pool. Did you see the way it worked the air currents coming off the water? We have our work cut out for ourselves this year if we're going to have a shot at the prize money," said Charlie.

Her expression was more awed than concerned. For a moment, Charlie felt a pang of jealousy at the way

Kelly was watching Caldwell chase down his plane. Then again, it was hard not to be impressed by both the kid and his paper airplane.

"Excuse me for a moment," Charlie said, and then he started after Caldwell. Crystal and Jeremy tried to come with him, but he waved them back. He figured he ought to make his introductions on his own. He didn't know what to expect from a kid who looked so slick, so mature—and if he was going to work his way in with this astronaut's son, he might have to do some pretty subtle acting. Crystal had a tendency to bludgeon her way through awkward situations, and Jeremy could be a loose cannon.

Charlie reached Caldwell just as he was bending to pick up the airplane from one of the paving stones.

"That was incredible," Charlie said, staring down at Caldwell's auburn hair. The strands were so shiny and straight, they could have belonged to an expensive doll. "Must have gone fifty feet. We'd be lucky if we could get one of our planes to cross Virginia Avenue!"

Charlie's comment wasn't that far from the truth. The few planes they'd made since Anastasia had sent in the paperwork to enter them into the competition had been crude flyers, barely better than the sort of four-fold paper airplanes kids like Dylan had been using to irritate homeroom teachers since the third grade. Though Charlie had taken a dozen books on the science of paper airplanes out of the library, and had been studying everything he could find online about the mechanics of paper flight, he and his team still had a lot to learn before they could consider themselves real competitors. Then again, from what Charlie had just witnessed, it was unlikely that any amount of library books or websites was going to prepare them to take on a kid like Richard Caldwell.

Caldwell grabbed the paper plane and rose to his feet, holding it out in front of Charlie. The orange light of a nearby streetlamp revealed perfect folds so crisp, the thing looked like it had been sculpted by a 3-D printer. Before Charlie could say anything, Caldwell was offering the plane to him.

"Feel free to take a closer look. It's my latest design. I brought it here for a test run because the water slows the air speed, simulates a bit of a vacuum."

Caldwell was smiling, the look on his face so friendly Charlie felt immediately bad that he wasn't just here making conversation with a fellow competitor. He was part of a scheme—for the second time in his life—and this time, the scheme could have real negative implications for this kid's father. Even if Buzz Caldwell was somehow involved in the theft of moon rocks, his son was innocent, just a smart kid who was particularly good at making paper airplanes.

"Wow, thanks. My name is Charlie, and that's my team over there. Except for the girl with the ponytail."

"Kelly. Yes, I recognize her from last year. She's got a real chance. If I remember correctly, her team had some pretty good designs. I think we beat them in the semis by a hair. If they kept at it during the off-season, they'll be real trouble this time around. Maybe even make it to the trophy. Then again, we haven't seen what you guys can do yet."

Caldwell was still smiling as Charlie took the plane into his hands. It was a far cry from anything he or the Whiz Kids had made.

"It's a whale of a competition," Caldwell continued. "Sometimes it's tough being the reigning champion, because you always want to outdo yourself the next year. There's a lot of expectations, a lot of pressure to win again. Man, I think my father has already cleared out space on his shelf for another trophy."

If anyone else had said the words, it might have sounded like bragging, but there was something so genuine and sincere about Caldwell, Charlie realized he was simply being honest. Charlie felt another pang of guilt;

this kid wasn't just smart and innocent—he was nice. And it appeared that his father had more than a passing interest in his kid's abilities; he was probably one of those dads that expected a lot from his son. Charlie was lucky that his own parents put very little pressure on him. He couldn't remember a single time when they'd hovered over him at some sort of competition, pushing him harder than he pushed himself. Then again, his parents were so absentminded and caught up in their own research, he'd have had to hit them over the head with a trophy just to let them know he had won it.

Charlie handed the airplane back to Caldwell.

"It's really great. I don't think you're going to have any trouble taking us down, with a design that good."

"You'll get there," Caldwell said. "A little hard work, a little practice. A lot of luck."

Judging from the precise nature of his airplane, and the fact that Caldwell had been practicing at the Reflecting Pool when all the other competitors had been at the opening reception banquet, Charlie guessed that Caldwell didn't leave very much up to luck. *Smart, nice, and dedicated.*

Charlie hoped Anastasia had her facts straight. Charlie considered himself a pretty good judge of character, and if first impressions meant anything, Richard

Caldwell didn't seem to have a dishonest bone in his body. It was hard to imagine that his father—the astronaut—was any different. Maybe Anastasia had it wrong; maybe Buzz Caldwell had nothing to do with the missing moon rocks, and this was all for nothing.

As Charlie thanked Caldwell again and headed back to Kelly and his team, he wondered if he was really going to be able to go through all of it. Getting close to Caldwell, just to find a way into his father's world.

Then again, to really get close to Caldwell, his team would have to stay in the competition as long as possible, hopefully all the way to the finals. Judging from what he'd just seen—that perfectly folded origami plane floating above the Reflecting Pool—he had a sinking feeling he and his friends would be on that Acela back to Boston sooner than Anastasia and her colleague might have expected.

Of course, that would mean no prize money—and no NASA.

Glancing back at Caldwell—who still had that amiable smile on his face, beneath those locks of auburn hair—Charlie convinced himself there was no real reason to feel bad about anything. Either they were going to lose the competition, fast and furious, and Anastasia would have to find another way to investigate Caldwell's dad, or they were going to somehow transform themselves into brilliant paper airplane designers, win cash prizes and introductions to NASA, and maybe even clear Caldwell's father's name in the process.

To Charlie, that sounded like win, win, and win. And heck, there would even be a nice shiny trophy involved. Win, win, win, and *win*.

9

TWELVE HOURS LATER, THE natural sunlight streaming in through the floor-to-ceiling windows of the main
atrium of the National Air and Space Museum chased
the last remnants of sleep from Charlie's eyes, as he
and his crew entered the Smithsonian's most popular
exhibit: Boeing Milestones of Flight Hall. Charlie's team
was already a few minutes late for the day's practice
trials—billed as their first chance to compete against
one of the other teams, even though it wouldn't count
as part of the actual competition—but it was impossible
to rush through a place filled with mankind's greatest
achievements in taming the skies. From the buzz and
chatter that surrounded Charlie, it appeared the other
competitors felt the same way; a hundred kids, as well

as a smattering of adult proctors, made for quite a noise. Even though the place was closed to the general public, Charlie had to shout just to be heard over the palpable, constant din.

"We're definitely in the right place. If you need to figure out how to make something fly, might as well start at the finish line and work your way back."

Charlie pointed toward the burnt-orange capsule standing directly across from the entrance, surrounded by kids taking pictures. Jeremy was already jogging toward the vessel, his gangly arms swinging excitedly by his sides. The Apollo 11 command module *Columbia* wasn't the most sophisticated spaceship in the atrium, but it was perhaps the most historical. Fifteen feet tall, vaguely pyramid in shape, it had once carried Neil Armstrong all the way to the moon and back. If modern flight had started with the first airplane built by the Wright brothers at Kitty Hawk—something every kid at Nagassack learned about at the start of middle school— it had surely reached its pinnacle with the first steps on the moon.

"Could you imagine being stuck in that thing for eighty hours?" Marion said, as they caught up to Jeremy at the back of the crowd around the capsule. "And we thought the four of us in one hotel room seemed cramped. Last night was positively palatial compared to space travel."

Charlie laughed. The previous night's accommodations had been tight: two of the boys to each of the two queen beds, and Crystal in her own room because she was the only girl. Crystal was bragging about her spacious extra bed, which didn't sit well with Kentaro. Of course, he could have slept on a throw pillow and had room to spare, but that hadn't kept him from complaining until well after two in the morning. One bathroom for four boys had ensured their late start even after Anastasia had sent Porter to pound on their doors at six a.m. Although Charlie could have skipped his shower—he didn't need cold water to help wake him up after seeing Porter's chiseled visage through the peephole. If that man ever smiled, it would be like a crack appearing in a glacial wall.

After a few minutes contemplating an eighty-hour trip to the moon in a sophisticated tin can, with Jeremy's elbow in his ear and Marion's feet jammed against his back, Charlie turned his attention to the exhibit directly behind the Apollo 11 capsule, the touchable moon rock. Ironic, to see the sample from the Apollo 17 journey to the moon, recovered from the landing site in the Taurus-Litrow Valley, set atop a pedestal for visitors to inspect and even touch. The humble appearance of the iron-rich, finely textured volcanic rock, basalt, did not reflect its true age, which was nearly four billion years. As first Jeremy, then Kentaro, Marion, and Crystal took turns touching the precious, priceless specimen, Charlie remembered back to the vial he had held in his hands. A piece of real history, the natural extension of human endeavor from the Wright brothers to the space program, a piece of the moon.

That was really why they were all there, in Washington. That was why they had spent the night sharing beds and dreaming about folding sheets of paper into airplanes—why Crystal had spent an entire hour before that watching YouTube videos of paper airplanes in flight, while Kentaro, Marion, Jeremy, and Charlie had folded sheet after sheet, thrown design after design toward the bathtub, the farthest distance they could reach without leaving their room.

Somebody had stolen moon rocks, and Charlie was going to help get them back.

"I'm glad you all finally decided to make an appearance." Anastasia's voice suddenly interrupted his thoughts, as she swept into view on the other side of the moon rock touch display. "I was beginning to think I'd have to send Mr. Porter to collect you. As you can imagine, Mr. Porter is not a particularly patient man."

Charlie detected a bit of venom in Anastasia's voice; the tone was alarming, especially considering up to that point she had been perfectly friendly, even charming. He wondered if something had changed—or perhaps it was just that she didn't like being kept waiting. Charlie's mother could get testy when his father was late—which was quite often—and she wasn't even involved in a NASA investigation.

"Sorry," Charlie said. "We were studying late. From what we've seen so far, it appears we're a bit less experienced than the other teams we've met."

He hadn't mentioned to Anastasia yet his impromptu meeting with Caldwell the night before; for some reason, he had decided to keep his impressions of the kid to himself, for the moment. He had no reason not to trust Anastasia, but he knew she already suspected Caldwell's father of being involved in a theft. He assumed that would color her opinion of the man's son, maybe unfairly.

"That's only natural," Anastasia said as she gestured for Charlie and his friends to follow her deeper into the atrium. "Considering they've all competed before."

Charlie had to jog to keep up with Anastasia's long gait. She'd traded her suit for black leggings and a black knit top with long sleeves, but her sunglasses were still covering much of her face, shielding her expression. Mr. Porter was nowhere to be seen, but Charlie guessed he was somewhere in the vicinity, perhaps watching from the second-floor landing.

"What do you mean?" Charlie asked. "I know Richard Caldwell has been here before, but I assumed some of the other teams were new to the competition, like us."

Passing beyond the touchable moon rock, they crossed between a pair of slightly older spacecraft. First up was the Gemini 4 capsule, which was encased in molded Plexiglas and perched right next to the actual space suit worn by astronaut Edward H. White. The plaque that bore his name and the date June 3, 1965, stated that he became the first American to perform a space walk. This was of note because he beat the Russian cosmonaut Alexei Leonov by three months. Next to Gemini 4 sat Mercury *Friendship 7*, a nine-foot-tall, 2,900-pound titanium vessel that had carried the first American to orbit the Earth, John H. Glenn Jr., back in 1962. Each one of these greats in flight symbolized a milestone of accomplishment.

"Yes, most of them are new to this competition. But they've all *competed* before."

Moving out of the Milestones of Flight Hall, they headed into a hallway labeled THE FLIGHT SIMULATOR WING. At the entrance to the hallway they passed beneath a pair of odd-looking vessels suspended from the ceiling by high-tensile metal wires. One of the vessels looked like the giant wings of some sort of mechanical butterfly, made of crisscrossing wooden beams. The other was a cross between a massive wooden biplane and the rounded base of a more modern blimp.

"The Lilienthal Glider and the Ecker Flying Boat," Anastasia commented, as Jeremy lifted Kentaro a few inches off the ground so he could get a better look. "Some early attempts at sustained flight."

"A boat with wings," Jeremy said, shaking his head. "Seems like a long way from that to a space capsule—"

"Hold on," Charlie interrupted. "Anastasia, what are you saying? All these other teams have competed before?"

Anastasia didn't slow her gait, taking them past a huge cavern of a room marked AMERICA BY AIR. The nose of a massive Boeing 747 sat a few yards inside the doorway. Marion had jogged ahead to stop just a few feet from a velvet rope in front of the towering nose. He quickly grabbed his drawing pad from his backpack and started to sketch what he was seeing. The motion of his hand was elegant and quick as he faithfully recreated the curves of the plane, leading up to where the cockpit would have been, if it hadn't simply been a model rather than the real thing.

"Great, Marion," Kentaro said. "If we can only figure out how to fold enough paper to make four, one-hundred-ten-thousand-horsepower engines, this will really help."

"Hey, you never know," Marion said. "Da Vinci started with sketches. Then he invented the helicopter."

"And five hundred years later someone actually built one that worked," Jeremy said.

"Quiet!" Charlie said. His voice rang out louder than he had intended, but still it didn't stop Anastasia from moving forward. She had reached the entrance to the practice hall, marked FLIGHT SIMULATION. Taking up an entire corner of the building, the space was massive, like a warehouse or an auditorium, big enough to contain twenty tables set up in five rows of four each. On the center of each table was a stack of white paper and five yellow wooden pencils. Most of the tables had already been claimed by various teams; Charlie could see the matching green backpacks of Worth Hooks down toward the far end of the room, and quickly picked out Richard Caldwell all the way near the front—right near the cordoned-off area where the competition would take place. Behind another velvet rope, similar to the one guarding the 747, Charlie saw a long stretch of polished-cement floor, marked off foot by foot. Although it was only a dozen yards wide, it had to be at least two hundred feet long—the length of two basketball courts, end to end.

"We're over here," Anastasia said, pointing to one of the few empty tables closest to the entrance. "There's enough paper to make as many airplanes as you need. Since this is a test run, you don't have to beat anyone, but there's certainly a psychological component to a game like this. You want to scare the other teams a little bit, make them question their own designs—"

"Wait," Charlie interrupted again, finally stopping Anastasia before she led them through the entrance. "What do you mean? How have all these other teams competed before?"

She turned back toward him. Her eyes were hidden behind those sunglasses.

"Didn't I tell you? All these other teams won their way into this competition in regional trials. It's a requirement on the entry forms."

Charlie felt something cold rising in his chest.

"If it's a requirement, then how are we here?"

There was a hint of a smile on Anastasia's thin lips.

"We faked your entry forms, of course."

With that, she turned and headed into the hall. Charlie stared at her, then quickly followed.

"You lied on the entry forms? And you didn't tell us?"

"Didn't have a choice," she said simply. "There was no time to get you into a regional challenge, and no way to ensure that you'd win a regional, anyway. So we doctored a few forms to make it look like your team won a local Newton/Brookline competition, and edged out two other nonexisting teams to win in a suburban-Boston regional. Our forms were good enough not to raise any red flags with the contest's governing committee; there are so many regions involved in the game, it was easy to slip one more onto the list. As far as the other teams believe, you're here because you won your way here."

As Charlie stared at her, she continued:

"Charlie, what we're doing is important. We had to do whatever was necessary to get you here."

She placed a hand on the small of his back and gave him a little shove toward the empty table. Before he could say anything, she was moving away, leaving his team alone with the stack of paper, the pencils, and the workbooks. Charlie was about to chase after her when Crystal leaned close to his ear.

"If we're going to have any chance at all here, we need to get to work."

"But you heard what she said, right?"

Crystal shrugged.

"There's not much we can do about it now. However she got us into the competition, we're here. And we don't want to embarrass ourselves, do we?"

Charlie's gaze shifted toward the far side of the room, where he'd spotted the Worth Hooks backpacks. He couldn't see Kelly from that distance, but he could imagine her bouncing ponytail. Crystal was right, of course. He would have to push away his concerns about Anastasia and the lies she had told to get them into the competition, at least for the moment.

He turned toward the stack of paper and started reaching for sheets. Then he noticed that Kentaro and Marion were already way ahead of him. The two of them were working together on a single sheet—Kentaro folding with his little, agile fingers while Marion read to him from a page in his sketchbook.

"You guys are really making a seven forty-seven?" Jeremy asked, coming around the other side of the table.

Kentaro had already folded the single page directly down the center. He carefully added two triangles from the tips.

"A seven forty-seven made out of paper would fly about as far as this building moves every time there's a light breeze. Simple aerodynamics, Jeremy. Or have you forgotten Professor Charlie's fabulous lecture?" said Kentaro.

Charlie blushed, but inside he was pleased that at least Kentaro had been listening. The "lecture" had taken place the night before, after they'd all brushed their teeth and readied themselves for bed. Charlie had decided the moment had been ripe to distill everything he had read, watched, and learned about flight in the preceding week since Anastasia had invited him to join the competition.

Simple aerodynamics. Kentaro was correct; that was the basic science behind all flight—not just paper airplanes, but big real ones, rocket ships, and even birds. Charlie remembered the way he had launched into his lecture, standing on one of the queen-size beds, his arm out at his side. He'd first held his hand out with his palm perpendicular to the ground, his thumb up in the air. Then he'd waved his arm back and forth like he was halfway into a loud clap. "All of you, give it a try," he'd said. Soon they had all been waving their arms like maniacs. "Feel the way the air pushes against your hand?" Then he'd turned his hand to the side, parallel to the floor, and the rest of the Whiz Kids had followed suit. "Now see how much easier it is to slide your arm through the air? Like slicing through warm butter. That, my friends, is aerodynamics at work."

From there, he'd launched into a discussion of the principles behind his actions—how the perpendicular facing of his hand had increased the drag, or resistance, by forcing the air against his flat palm. For a plane to fly properly for a long distance, you had to find a way to shape it so it decreased the drag as much as possible. And then you needed to take into account the force of gravity—the inexorable pull downward—through the principles of thrust and lift. Thrust was the action of his muscles sending his arm forward, lift was the way his horizontal palm made the air push upward against his skin. Four scientific forces working together to keep his hand moving forward. Four scientific forces that would work together to keep any object in the air—a bird, a spaceship, a jumbo jet, a paper airplane.

"Four forces in balance," Kentaro said, folding the tip of the paper down and creasing the top. "Resistance, gravity, lift, thrust. The goal is to focus a little more on the lift—if it glides more slowly, it will travel farther. Simple physics."

He brought the sides in symmetrically, and after a

few more folds, his plane was complete. He held it high in the air. It was mostly rectangular, with a flat nose and a squarish body. It wasn't pretty or sleek, nothing like the elegant, perfect plane Caldwell had flown over the Reflecting Pool, or the long, thin plane Ryan had tossed through the train car. In fact, it wasn't something you would think could fly more than a few feet.

"This morning, while you guys were fighting over the shower, I watched a kid make this one on a Japanese website. I don't think people will understand the Japanese name so let's just call it the *Nagassack Ninja*."

He handed the plane to Charlie. It felt a little front heavy, a little short in the wings. But Kentaro looked confident.

"That's what you've come up with? Looks like a milk carton with wings. It's going to be too easy for the other team to beat us," said Charlie.

"Give it a nice smooth throw and you'll see. It packs a heck of a punch."

Kentaro pointed to the testing area. Kids were already lining up in two rows to try out their various planes against each other, team versus team. Charlie decided it wouldn't hurt to give Kentaro's plane a chance. After all, they didn't really have anything better to work with.

He moved past the row of tables and took his position at the end of one of the lines. Kentaro and Jeremy came with him; Marion and Crystal remained behind at the table, folding more sheets of paper and checking out the various sketches in Marion's drawing pad. As Charlie waited for the line to move forward, he surveyed the planes in front of him and in the line across from him. So many variations, so many different folding styles. He knew they were all working with the same four scientific principles—resistance, gravity, thrust, lift—but there seemed to be so many different ways to attack the problem. This wasn't like math at all, where usually there was one right answer. There seemed to be hundreds of right answers, and just as many that could very well be wrong. Charlie looked down at Kentaro's *Nagassack Ninja*.

"I don't know, Kentaro. I just don't know," Charlie said. Then he raised his eyes to see Ryan standing in the line directly across from him. Apparently, the big redhead had pushed his way ahead of a dozen other kids to make sure he'd be competing directly with Charlie in the test run. Some of the other kids looked like they wanted to complain, but since Ryan stood a head taller than all of them, they offered up nothing but angry looks.

"It's just a trial run," Jeremy said. "We've got something much better in store for the real competition."

Kentaro kicked at Jeremy's shin, but Jeremy ignored the little neon sneaker, giving Charlie a last push forward to the test area starting line. The next thing Charlie knew, he was standing side by side with Ryan, a crowd of kids on either side of them counting down.

"Three . . . two . . . one!"

Charlie hooked his arm back and threw, trying to keep his hand as steady and smooth as possible. Out of the corner of his eye he could see Ryan heaving his own plane forward, his longer arm offering so much more strength and thrust, and then the two competing planes were off, flying directly down the test track.

Ryan's plane—almost twice as long as the *Ninja*, tapered to a fine, sharp point—took off faster, slicing through the air like a horizontal rocket. But Charlie was pleased to see the *Ninja* was at least flying straight, rising slightly upward as it slowly drifted down the long lane, passing over the distance markers one after another.

"Look at it go!" Kentaro yelled. "Make Daddy proud, little *Ninja*!"

"Little ninja?" Ryan shouted back. "There's nothing little about that pig. Talk about a flying boat."

Charlie ignored Ryan's taunts, focused on the two planes as they continued down the track. Ryan's was way ahead now, but it was starting to descend, ever so slightly. Another minute and it was going to touch down. The *Ninja* was way behind, but going strong, still rising ever so slightly. For a moment Charlie really believed they had a shot at winning. . . .

And then the *Ninja* started to wobble in the air. Almost imperceptibly at first, then harder, until it was trembling like a dog coming inside after a cold rain.

"Uh-oh, Daddy," Ryan said. "Your little ninja is having an epileptic fit."

"What's happening?" Jeremy asked.

"It's gotten too slow," Charlie said. "The forces are out of balance. Gravity overcoming thrust, and now it's giving in to the drag. Down it goes."

And down it went. Straight down, down, down, hitting the ground nose-first. Someone nearby shouted out a number—thirty-seven—the distance in feet. Thirty-seven feet. Pretty good for a first try, but nowhere near a competitive distance, from what Charlie had seen so far. Another ten seconds went by, and then Ryan's plane finally drifted down out of the air.

"Eighty-nine!" someone shouted. Ryan grimaced.

"Not my best showing. Anything under a hundred gets the shredder."

Then he turned to face Charlie, a cruel smile on his lips.

"Don't know what the heck Kelly sees in you bozos. The scent of loser coming off you is enough to make me puke."

He gave Charlie a thumbs-down and headed back toward where the other Worth Hooks kids were waiting, clapping their hands at his easy win. Charlie caught sight of Kelly in the group of green backpacks, but she avoided his gaze. Charlie turned and headed back toward his team's table. Anastasia was waiting for him, standing stiffly between Crystal and Marion, who were busily folding more paper airplanes.

"I wouldn't call that an auspicious start, would you, Charlie?"

"It's not like we had a fair chance," Charlie responded, more angry than he wanted to be. "We're brand-new to this. Everyone else here has won contests before; everyone here knows how to fold a darn paper airplane."

Crystal and Marion looked up from their planes. Jeremy and Kentaro had gone still behind Charlie, watching him. Anastasia waited a full beat before lowering her sunglasses to show her green eyes.

"I chose you because you're supposed to be special, Charlie. You're as smart as any kid here—smarter than most. So maybe you're starting a few feet behind the line; you're supposed to be smart enough to make up the difference."

She turned and headed toward the door, where Charlie saw the menacingly large shape of Mr. Porter. He waited until she was gone from sight before turning back to his friends. Crystal and Marion had gone back to their folding, and Jeremy and Kentaro were watching other teams taking turns at the testing track. Nobody was saying anything, but Charlie knew what they were all thinking.

Everyone had been telling Charlie he was a genius for as long as he could remember, but for the first time in a long, long while, he didn't feel all that smart. Kentaro's *Nagassack Ninja* had flown okay, but it was nowhere near good enough to compete with the other planes in the competition.

Maybe Charlie had been wrong when he'd first surveyed the exhibits in the great hall of the Air and Space Museum. Maybe starting at the finish line was the wrong approach.

These other teams had all competed before. They

were already ready to make Apollo capsules and head for the moon. But Charlie's team was starting from scratch. From less than scratch. As Anastasia had said, they weren't even at the starting line yet. They weren't the Apollo space project; they weren't astronauts.

They were Wilbur and Orville Wright. And if they were going to have any chance in this competition, they needed to go back to the very beginning.

"I CAN SEE WHY they chose this place," Kentaro squealed, his face inches from a rattling square of glass overlooking a stretch of sand that ran horizontal to the asphalt parking lot. "This wind gets any stronger, this bus is going to be airborne too!"

"From flying boats to flying buses," Jeremy chimed in from the seat ahead of Kentaro. "If we can just work our way to planes, we'll be in business."

Charlie ignored Jeremy's facetious comment. Kentaro had it right, he thought, looking out the window from his own seat, halfway down the near empty bus they'd been trapped inside for the long five-and-a-half-hour trip from Washington, DC, to Kitty Hawk.

They had chosen the famous location from the list

of possible field trips that each team had been given when they'd checked in to the competition. Charlie could tell by the sparseness of the bus that they were the only team that had picked what had to be the farthest excursion, distance-wise, but he didn't care: He could see firsthand many of the reasons Orville and Wilbur Wright had made the choice of the Atlantic-beachfront testing ground for their first attempts at heavier-than-air flight. The frequent, gusty winds. The fact that the nearby North Carolina town had been home to less than sixty families back in 1900, when the Wright brothers had practiced their craft. And maybe most important, nearby small, rolling hills and soft sands for when something, inevitably, went wrong.

The bus pulled to a creaking stop at the edge of the parking lot, and Anastasia signaled the kids to file out. Mr. Porter stared down at the kids menacingly as they walked past him. Charlie wasn't sure if that was his intention, or if it simply had to do with the way his eyebrows were shaped. Charlie followed Jeremy, Kentaro, Crystal, and Marion outside. There were only three other tourists.

"Feel that Atlantic Ocean breeze," Crystal said, once they'd all made it off the bus and were strolling past the Wright Brothers National Memorial Visitor Center.

"We don't have much time here, so let's be efficient about this excursion," Anastasia said. Porter nodded in agreement.

Charlie shielded his eyes as he surveyed the area: sunlight streaming around the Wright Monument at the top of Big Kill Devil Hill flashed like the beam of a lighthouse. Past the monument, there was just a long, rolling swath of sand and hills. He watched as a single seagull flapped past, wings fighting against the breeze, a vision of feather and beak circumnavigating the monument in an elegant arc.

"Hard to imagine," he said, "but when the Wright brothers set up shop here, flight was something reserved for birds."

It was a compelling moment, standing in that historical spot. During the bus ride, they'd had a lot of time to go over the Wright brothers' journey to a working plane, reading from a trio of books Crystal had downloaded from the Internet onto her phone. From 1900 to 1903, the brothers had tried many iterations of their glider design, finally ending up with the Wright Flyer, which would become their first manned vessel. It wasn't until December 14, 1903, that—after winning a coin toss to determine who would fly first—Wilbur had set out in the entirely spruce-built plane. He'd taken off from a launching rail they had crafted running down one of the nearby hills—the ominously named Big Kill Devil Hill—for a gravity-assisted takeoff. That plane had left the rail but had only remained airborne for a matter of seconds, crashing to the sand and suffering minor damage. Three days later, on December 17, 1903, it had been Orville's turn. With wind speeds well over twenty miles per hour, the conditions had been even more perfect—and his first flight had lasted twelve seconds, his plane flying 120 feet.

From there, the Wright brothers had continued to take turns, flying a total of four times. Wilbur's last flight had clocked in at 852 feet, staying aloft for fifty-nine seconds. The front elevator supports had been damaged upon that last landing, and seconds after Wilbur had gotten off the thing, a strong wind had tossed the Flyer across the sand like a toy, damaging it beyond repair.

After passing the monument and the seagull, the Whiz Kids crossed in front of the reconstructed hangar and original workshop of the brothers. Anastasia and Porter followed behind them. The place was quiet—only a handful more tourists than the trio that had accompanied them on the bus—which made sense, since it was the middle of the day in the middle of the week. Normally, Charlie and his friends would have been in school, lodged somewhere between sixth-period science and seventh-period social studies. Charlie would have been contemplating the jog between classes through the long Nagassack hallways, using the banks of lockers as natural obstructions as he tried to avoid Dylan Wigglesworth and his coterie of thugs.

Even the thought of Dylan, his hometown tormenter, gave Charlie a little burst of adrenaline, and he hurried his step as he passed the hangar. And caught sight of a huge, five-foot-tall boulder supporting an enormous bronze plaque.

"There it is," he said excitedly. "The First Flight Boulder. Over a hundred years ago, this was the very spot where the Flyer lifted off."

Charlie's pulse was rocketing as he reached the bronze plaque and ran his fingers over the raised letters that told the story of that famous first flight. As the rest of his friends reached the boulder, Charlie turned and looked down the long, grated pathway that stretched out ahead of him along the sandy bluff, running the entire distance of the Flyer's first flights. He could see other boulders set along the pathway, marking the Wright brothers' earlier attempts, each engraved with details indicating the progress from design to implementation.

Charlie paused, letting his mind go blank, as the

ocean breeze pulled at his clothes. This was where it had all started. This was the place he had come for answers, and he really believed those answers were somehow hidden in that long stretch of sand.

Before he truly knew what he was doing, he stretched his arms out at his sides like airplane wings. Then he took off down the grated path, quickly accelerating to a full run. Jeremy shouted something behind him, but he was moving too fast now, the air whizzing past his ears. Faster, faster, faster, his chest heaving, his legs pumping, his feet slamming against the grates. The next marker grew bigger and bigger, closer and closer— and then finally he reached the four-foot-high stone. He skidded to a stop, breathing hard, and just as before ran his fingers along the engraved words.

END OF 1ST FLIGHT

TIME: 12 SECONDS

DISTANCE: 120 FT

DEC. 17, 1903

PILOT: ORVILLE

"Charlie!" Jeremy shouted.

Charlie looked back and saw that Jeremy and Crystal were now running the same path behind him, their arms straight out at their sides. Anastasia and Porter looked like tiny specks in the distance. Kentaro and Marion had hung behind too, most likely heading to the gift shop: Kentaro had a thing for cheap tchotchkes. Looking at Jeremy and Crystal and the way they moved was a lesson in itself; their bodies were so different—Jeremy's long arms and legs spindly like half-cooked spaghetti, Crystal more compact and sure of herself, every now and then using one of her wings to make sure her glasses didn't get blown off her face. Two very different designs, flying the same path, at nearly the same speed.

Four forces in balance in very different ways. The thrust of their churning legs, the drag of the wind against their bodies. Gravity pulling them both against the grated pathway, lift provided by their outstretched arms.

"We can do this," Charlie whispered to himself.

And then he turned and started forward again, heading for the second stone marker. Arms still out, he was transported 114 years back in time. He was the Wright Flyer zipping through the air, just a few yards over the sand, moving faster and farther than any heavier-than-air object built by man before. *We can do this.*

The Wright Flyer was made of spruce wood, with an engine. All they had to work with was paper. *But maybe that's the key.* Charlie closed on the second marker. He yelled back over his shoulder to Jeremy and Crystal, who were still behind him.

"Twelve seconds, one hundred and seventy-five feet!"

He ignored the spots that were starting to float in his vision as his lungs burned from the effort. The third marker came up even faster.

"Fifteen seconds, two hundred feet! I'm going all the way!"

Crystal and Jeremy kept running after him. They were a dozen yards behind, chugging along. Charlie wasn't faster than either of them, but at the moment, he was like a man possessed. His outstretched arms glided through the air, as thin as he could make them to cut down on the drag and add to the lift. His legs pumped and pumped, thrust against gravity.

Finally, he could make out the fourth marker in the distance. Closer and closer and closer. His mind was really gone now, whirling back in time. It had taken the Wright brothers four flights to find the right synergy between the four forces. They had used a metal rail as a guide, had gotten the wings and weight and angle just right. And then they had experimented with materials, ending up with mostly spruce. Then, after their success, they shifted to an even more stable and more malleable wood, white pine. That was the key. *Not just the four forces, but the material.*

Charlie skidded to a heaving stop next to the final stone marker.

"Fifty-nine seconds," he gasped, reading what the Wright brothers had achieved. "Eight hundred and fifty-two feet."

It was another minute before Jeremy and Crystal reached him, and crumpled to the sand. Jeremy's long body looked like a giant Portuguese man-of-war jellyfish that had floated up from the beach. Crystal had her glasses off, wiping sweat from her brow.

"What the heck was that?" she huffed. "Have you gone completely mental on us? You know you're not an airplane, right?"

Charlie grinned.

"It's the materials, Crystal."

She looked at him.

"We can't change our materials. The rules limit us to paper. Twenty-pound letter size, to be exact."

"That's right. We're limited to paper. But that doesn't mean we can't change the *materials*."

"He *has* gone mental," Jeremy said.

"No, listen. There *is* a way to change the materials. By changing the way we fold the paper. If we can simulate a lighter paper in certain areas like the wings, and simulate heavier paper in the nose area, by using strategic folds, we can pull this off."

Crystal slowly put her glasses back on her face. Then

a smile crept across her lips. She, better than anyone, understood how different materials exhibited different properties. Different types of rocks had different densities, different levels of porousness, different reactions to heat. Sandstone could be smelted into glass, carbon could be crushed into diamond. And just maybe, paper could be folded into something approximating spruce or pine.

Slowly the three of them headed back toward the visitor center. As Charlie had suspected, they found Marion and Kentaro exiting the gift shop. Porter stood near the entrance of the store cleaning his sunglasses with a silky black cloth. Anastasia motioned for the kids to return to the bus. Kentaro waved a small silver-and-gray model airplane in the air, the words KITTY HAWK 1903 inked across the fuselage.

"What's that for?" Charlie asked.

"Well, I figure one way or another we go home with an airplane-shaped trophy."

Charlie grinned as Kentaro stuck the model airplane into his neon backpack.

He felt certain now: One way or another, they sure were going to go home with that trophy.

"ONE HUNDRED AND EIGHTY-THREE. One hundred and eighty-four. One hundred and eighty-five! A new record!"

Charlie watched the opposing team's *Flying Fox* design touch down next to the distance marker with a sinking feeling in his stomach, as the crowd around him erupted in applause. Maybe letting the other team throw first had been a mistake; a throw like that was going to be almost impossible to beat, and it suddenly felt like the Whiz Kids' remarkable day was finally heading toward a disappointing end.

Charlie tried to ignore the continuing applause aimed at the opposing team—a group of girls from Ms. Fine Parker Academy in Jacksonville, Florida—as he approached the starting line. Eight hours into the day of competition, the crowd had been whittled down from over a hundred kids to fewer than forty; only eight teams remained, and the winner of each of these trials was going to be on their way to the semifinals. The fact that Charlie's team had made it this far had stunned the crowd—most of all Anastasia and Porter, who were standing at the back of the room. Anastasia had actually even smiled a few times, though Charlie still hadn't seen any evidence that Porter's face had the ability to show emotion.

But all of that seemed like it was about to come to an ignoble end. The lessons Charlie and his team had learned at Kitty Hawk had enabled them to create planes that had gone over a hundred feet—four times in six hours, actually, but they'd never gotten anywhere near 185. The *Flying Fox* was an amazing design—hefty at the front, but with long wings and drag-reducing "ears" that gave it its name. The girl who had made the throw, almost a head taller than Charlie, with long brown pigtails and denim overalls, was too busy celebrating with her teammates to even notice Charlie as he took his place next to her at the starting line. Unlike the practice sessions, in the real competition the contestants took turns throwing, which seemed fortuitous at the moment. Judging from his last few throws, his plane would have been eating the *Flying Fox*'s exhaust.

One hundred and eighty-five: only forty-two feet shy of the Guinness World Record flight set back in 2012 by John M. Collins and Joe Ayoob. Collins was an aircraft designer who had perfected a sleek paper airplane design, and then had called in Ayoob, a former California-Berkeley quarterback, to make the throw. Ayoob had thrown the plane so hard during practice runs, it had almost shredded in the air, but eventually he made the record-winning distance.

As Charlie stood at the starting line, raising his twig-like right arm, his team's so-far-unbeaten design held gently in his fingers, he knew there was no chance of anything being shredded today. He didn't have a quarter-back's arm strength; he barely had the arm strength of a sixth grader. His plane's thrust would be limited to whatever his feeble muscles could muster, amplified by the torque of a hopefully perfect throw.

At least the plane in his fingers was something of a work of art. Artistically designed by Marion, mathematically calculated by himself with Jeremy's help, folded by Kentaro, and measured and weighed by Crystal, it was truly the result of team effort. Charlie knew that the plane was as close to perfect as they could manage.

Working off of his epiphany at Kitty Hawk, they'd used precise folds to mimic different materials in different parts of the plane. The nose was made heavy and thick, pine or even maple, made by tripling and quadrupling the paper toward the tip; the wings were long and light, balsa or spruce, just single sheets. The tail was almost as sharp as the front, but half its weight. They'd gone over the calculations in their room until three in the morning, and when they'd hit the competition, they'd proved their calculations from the very first flight.

But now all of that seemed irrelevant. As the crowd finally quieted down behind him, Charlie stared down the long track; 185 feet was so far ahead of him, he couldn't even make out the marker. Such a throw seemed impossible.

"Come on, Charlie," he heard from behind him. "You can do this." Crystal and Jeremy were only a few feet away, Crystal leaning forward so her whisper could be heard over the low, expectant murmur from the crowd. "We've got the design down. Now it's all about the math."

Charlie knew exactly what she meant. The plane was beautiful; now its flight was going to come down entirely to his release. And as much as a paper airplane throw seemed to be about muscle strength and athleticism, it was really about math. Angles and force, calculated as exactly as possible.

Charlie had run the numbers himself. He knew that he needed to release the plane at a thirty-six-degree angle to the ground to allow the plane's design to best overcome the force of gravity and reach the optimum flying height. He had to use the circular spin of his arm with just the right amount of centrifugal force needed to overcome enough drag to keep the plane aloft long enough for it to complete a parabolic arc.

Charlie took a deep breath, trying to steady his hand. He looked down the long track one more time—and in the edge of his vision caught sight of Kelly, standing with her team right past the ten-foot marker. She nodded at him, her blond ponytail bobbing with the motion. She believed in him. He just needed to believe in himself.

Math. Numbers. This was his world.

He drew his arm back as far as he could, then whirled it forward, fast as a snapping rubber band. He released at the tip of the arc, as close to thirty-six degrees as he could manage. Then he closed his eyes.

For the first few seconds he heard nothing; the crowd had gone dead quiet, the room frozen like Massachusetts in February. Then he began to hear surprised whispers, followed by outright gasps.

He opened his eyes. The plane was still in the air, still rising. But it was moving slowly—so incredibly slowly, it almost seemed like a special effect. The other kids had never seen anything like it. The heaviness of the plane's nose, the length of its tail, the sharpness of its wings—the way they'd mimicked other materials with folds of paper—were combining to make the plane stay in the air well beyond what seemed possible.

"Wow," Crystal whispered from behind Charlie. "Look at it go."

Look at it go. The plane floated past the ninety-foot marker and kept on going, rising incrementally. At ninety-five, it seemed to level off, but it wasn't until a hundred feet that it started to inch downward, beginning the descent portion of the parabola. *My god*, Charlie thought. *It just might make it. It just might*—

And then something happened. Maybe it was a draft of air from a vent in the high ceilings, maybe it was some infinitesimal dust particles floating through the vast hall, but the plane's descent began to accelerate. The nose dipped slightly downward, and then the plane was descending faster and faster.

"Oh no," someone in the crowd gasped. "It's going down!"

Charlie's eyes widened. He couldn't believe it was

happening. They had gotten so close. He watched as the plane slid lower and lower in the air. Then he looked at the markers below. A hundred and ten feet. A hundred and fifteen. A hundred and twenty.

"I can't watch," Jeremy hissed from next to Crystal. "I can't—"

"Wait," Crystal said. "Look!"

Charlie raised his eyes back to the plane—and was shocked to see it had somehow leveled off. The long wings had stabilized in the air, and the tip was now horizontal with the floor. The plane was a bare five feet off the floor, but it was still going forward! It passed the 150 marker and kept on going. Straight as an arrow. Cutting through the air, still in slow motion, but ever forward.

One sixty. One sixty-five. One seventy. One seventy-five.

And finally, it started going downward again, but this time slowly, gently. As if there was a tiny pilot inside, aiming for a perfect, soft landing.

"One eighty-five," the crowd yelled. "One eighty-six. One eighty-seven. One eighty-eight!!"

The plane touched down and skidded to a stop. There was a brief pause. Then the crowd erupted again, even louder than before. Charlie felt hands patting his shoulders, and he turned and hugged Crystal, then Jeremy. He could see Kentaro and Marion leaping up and down at their table, Kentaro's head barely visible at the peak of each excited jump.

Charlie released Crystal and Jeremy, and took a step back. He found himself searching the crowd for Kelly but didn't see her. He was about to head back to their table when he felt another hand on his shoulder. He expected Jeremy, but to his surprise, he found himself facing Richard Caldwell. Caldwell smiled and gave Charlie's shoulder a warm pat.

"Fantastic," Caldwell said. "You definitely deserve the award for most improved. A hundred and eighty-eight feet, that's a new track record. Last year I won with a hundred and eighty-four."

Charlie didn't know what to say. He would have expected jealousy, or at least some competitive edginess, but Caldwell seemed completely sincere. Charlie finally managed an embarrassed shrug.

"We got lucky, I think. Maybe there was a breeze helping us along."

"You got good, not lucky. You left here in last place, came back in first. Tomorrow, there are just four teams left. You guys. The bunch from Worth Hooks. A team from a prep school in Dallas. And my team."

Caldwell tilted his head toward a group of four boys watching from two tables away. "Which means I'll be seeing you at the dinner tonight, right?"

"Dinner?"

"It's a tradition we started when we won two years ago. My father's company, Aerospace Infinity, hosts the dinner at my family's house. AI cosponsors the competition as well, and puts up the cash prize."

"Your father has an aerospace company?"

Caldwell smiled. "Being an astronaut is cool, but you can't do it forever. He's been in the aerospace business for years now. The company is mostly into developing new materials for spaceflight, like new metals for heat shields on rockets and new types of glass for the windows on the International Space Station. That sort of thing."

"That's so neat," Charlie said. Then he had a thought. "Your father hosts the semifinalists dinner. What if you didn't make it?"

Caldwell shrugged.

"I guess we'll cross that bridge if we come to it. Like I told you before, my dad is pretty hard-core; he expects a lot from me. You should have heard his lecture when I once brought home a B in second-grade math."

Charlie whistled. He felt bad for Caldwell, although he doubted Caldwell had gotten many Bs in his lifetime.

"Well, thanks for the invite; we'll definitely be there."

Caldwell nodded, then returned to his own team. Charlie headed toward his friends, holding an invitation out in front of him.

"Crystal, get your party shoes ready."

Before he could reach them, Anastasia stepped between him and the rest of the Whiz Kids. In a swift, sudden motion, she took the invite out of his hand.

"Not so fast. I've got another invitation for the five of you before the dinner."

"This afternoon?" Charlie said. "I figured we needed to practice some more, for the semis and finals."

Both events were scheduled for tomorrow—the semis in the morning, the finals in the afternoon. Charlie's team had done amazingly well. As Caldwell had said, they currently held the record for the best flight in tournament history. But Charlie had only been half joking when he'd told Caldwell it was probably luck. He himself still had no idea how he'd gotten the plane to go so far.

"Practice is important," Anastasia said. "But you've shown me today, as I'd hoped all along, you have the skill and the innate abilities. There's really only one thing I think you might be missing."

Charlie raised his eyebrows. Jeremy moved next to him, gesturing toward Caldwell's crew. "Better haircuts?"

Anastasia didn't smile. Her expression remained unreadable behind her sunglasses.

"Motivation," she said simply, as she slid the invitation into the pocket of her tailored jacket.

12

EYES CLOSED, IT WAS just a lot of paper. Stacks of hand-size paper, piled across a two-foot-by-three-foot pallet, sealed together by strips of cellophane. Barely an inch tall in most places, smelling vaguely of damp moss. Just a whole lot of paper—about ten pounds, if Charlie had to guess, heavy enough to make his arms quiver as he tried not to drop the darn thing.

But when he finally opened his eyes, to multiple flashes from Kentaro's disposable camera—heck, who even knew where to *find* a disposable camera anymore— it almost took Charlie by surprise to see the green faces staring up at him from beneath the cellophane. Eyes open, it wasn't just paper. It was stack after stack of twenty-dollar bills.

A quarter of a million dollars in twenties, to be precise, more than Charlie had ever seen in one place in his lifetime. A true fortune. Awed by what he was holding, Charlie struggled against the weight of the pallet; luckily Crystal stepped in at the last minute to keep the thing from tumbling to the floor. Over her head, Charlie could see Marion and Kentaro sitting next to each other cross-legged on the floor, both of them laughing at him as Kentaro continued snapping photos. Jeremy would have probably poked fun at his pathetic, diminutive *Tyrannosaurus rex*–like arms, if he hadn't been standing so close to the uniformed tour guide, who was still going over the history of the place with Anastasia. Anastasia, for her part, was still wearing her sunglasses, but at least she had left Mr. Porter waiting outside in the black SUV that had transported them all there from the Watergate.

"I think we get the idea," Crystal said loudly toward the guide, while helping Charlie put the pallet of twenties back on the display table at the center of the room. "A quarter million dollars is heavier than it looks."

The guide separated himself from Jeremy and Anastasia, then gestured for the group to head back out into the floral-carpeted hallway that led deeper into the high-ceilinged facility.

Charlie followed his team out of the room, wondering to himself what it would be like to work in a factory were you literally printed money every day. The Bureau of Engraving and Printing might not have been on most people's lists of things to do in Washington, DC, but Charlie had found the place fascinating from the moment Anastasia had led them through the front entrance and past the multiple metal detectors and security posts that guarded the interior of the plant. Charlie wasn't certain why Anastasia had brought them there during a few hours that the competition had set aside that afternoon for sightseeing; Charlie could think of a half dozen other places in the nation's capital that might have made more sense, from a tourist's point of view. But Anastasia had made it clear on the trip over that right now they were anything but tourists.

Now that they were deep on the inside, traveling through a wide, column-lined hallway with canted metal ceilings resembling the arched framework of an airplane hanger, Charlie felt like they were descending into a secret, underground world. The fluorescent bulbs dangling above his head reminded him of some sort of World War II bunker, though he guessed the fixtures, along with the flowery carpeting below his feet, were more likely the product of a 1970s makeover of the tourist-approved sections of the factory. But even so, as they moved past doors leading to the printing presses themselves, where sheet after sheet of bills of every denomination sped across conveyer belts and curled around giant spools to be inked, pressed, sliced, and eventually put into circulation, Charlie got the sense that in here, time moved a little differently than in the outside world. The men and women who worked in this plant, surrounded by a potential fortune measured in the billions and trillions, had to be a special breed.

Charlie watched the guide as he led them out of the hallway and into a circular room at the dead center of the E-shaped facility, and wondered, did the man ever feel tempted to try to take his work home with him? Print up a few extra sheets of hundreds for himself?

Of course, such a crime would be nearly impossible. Looking up past the fluorescent bulbs, Charlie could see that there were cameras everywhere. Little black, buglike eyes, reminiscent of the security he'd seen deep inside Incredo Land. If a theme park had had tight security, he imagined that the place where all of America's money was minted would function on a whole different plane altogether.

"Okay, friends," the guide said as he led them toward the middle of the circular room. "This is most people's favorite part of the tour."

He pointed toward a large glass cube, about three feet tall and wide, held up by four cast-iron legs. As Charlie approached, he noticed a fair amount of wear and scratches across the glass—the thing had been touched by many many hands over the years. Once he saw what was inside, he understood.

"A million dollars," the guide continued, "in ten-dollar bills."

Charlie pressed in next to Crystal and Jeremy at one side of the case, while Kentaro and Marion hovered over the other.

"Now, that would make a nice coffee table," Jeremy said. "I wonder if these legs are bolted to the floor."

"If Charlie couldn't carry a quarter million in twenties," Crystal said. "I doubt you'd get two inches before this flattened you like a pancake."

Kentaro pointed to his ever-present neon backpack, hanging from his left shoulder.

"How about just a little goodie bag? I could buy a lot more toy planes with a few inches of freshly printed green."

The guide strolled past them, toward another hallway. Charlie heard a loud whirring from the guide's direction and saw beyond the man's uniformed shoulders that the hallway ahead of him was lined by glass windows overlooking one of the money printing presses. Even from that distance, he could see the sheets of green speeding along the press, a blur of untold fortunes.

Kentaro, Marion, Jeremy, and Crystal moved after the guide, toward the presses. Charlie was about to follow when he felt Anastasia's hand on his shoulder, holding him back.

"Let's stay here for a moment and talk, Charlie."

She came around to the other side of the million-dollar cube, placing her palms flat against the scratched glass.

"You're probably wondering why I brought you here."

Charlie shrugged. "I assume that seeing all this money is supposed to make us think about the prize money we could win."

Anastasia drummed her fingernails against the glass.

"That's partly correct. Money can be a great moti-vation. Although I don't think you're here because of the money, are you? There are many other teams in the competition who would benefit much more from win-ning the cash prize."

Charlie thought about Kelly and the team from New Haven, even Ryan. It was true—money wasn't really that important to Charlie. He'd learned that lesson before: that for all its temptations, money could be more trouble than it was worth. Friendships and people always trumped money.

"Money, Charlie, that's just paper. Printed like pages in a book."

"NASA," Charlie said, eyeing his friends as they moved farther down the hallway, toward those printing presses. For some reason, Charlie really wanted nothing more than to chase his friends down the hall to get away from Anastasia. She didn't seem at all like the fascinating, friendly—if mysterious—woman who had first come to him at Nagassack to ask for his help. There was something much more frightening and determined about her now. "We're really excited to have a chance to make a good impression with your organization. We all want to be scientists when we grow up."

Anastasia nodded, her fingers still bouncing against the case.

"Closer," she said. Then she seemed to change tack. "You know, they ought to have put some of these bills facing the other way, because the thing about money, and impressions, is that there are always two sides to them. Heads or tails, dead presidents and important buildings. A good recommendation to a government space agency—or a charge of perjury for lying on an official document to enter a national contest to win a cash prize."

Charlie felt his entire chest grow cold. He stared at Anastasia. "What?"

"You heard me. You lied on your applications to enter this contest."

Charlie took a step back from the glass case. "We didn't lie. *You* did."

Anastasia smiled beneath her sunglasses. "Me? I'm just a proctor. I'm not on the verge of getting to the finals and potentially winning that cash prize. And I think you'll find that the signatures on your applications look pretty familiar. You can argue about it all you want, and maybe the contest authorities will believe you, or maybe they won't. Either way, I doubt NASA will take your word over mine, considering I was an engineer there for many years."

Charlie's eyes narrowed. The anger was boiling up inside of him. "What do you want from us? We made it to the semifinals. I've befriended Richard Caldwell."

"And tonight you're going to dinner at his father's house. It will be the perfect opportunity to begin looking for evidence of the missing moon rocks."

Charlie swallowed, hard. "You want us to snoop around his house, during dinner?"

"You'll gain access to his private study, while the other kids are busy with the appetizers. Once inside, you'll go through his desk, filing cabinets, whatever might contain information that isn't left out in the open."

Charlie had known all along that he had entered the contest to help find the moon rocks, but this was something different. This was sneaking around an astronaut's house, breaking into his study. This was unethical. And probably illegal.

Charlie wished he had never kept the real reason he had entered the competition from his father; he wished he could call his dad now and explain about the moon rocks, tell him how Anastasia had faked their applications and was now threatening to use that against them. His father would certainly believe him, but would it help? If Anastasia had really faked his signature, which wouldn't have been too difficult for a former NASA engineer, it would be Charlie's word against hers.

"Who do you really work for?" Charlie asked. "You're not with NASA, even if you used to be. And I don't think you're with any governmental organization, or law enforcement. Why do you want these moon rocks?"

Anastasia tapped her fingernails against the glass

one last time, then took a step backward toward the hallway leading to the printing presses.

"We better rejoin the tour," she said, instead of answering. "There isn't much time to get you and your friends back to the hotel to get dressed for dinner. And Charlie . . ." She looked him up and down, then sighed. "Try to wear something nice. The Caldwell family is one of the most esteemed in all of Washington. You don't want to show up looking like some kid sent to mow their front lawn."

With that, she turned and headed after the tour guide.

Charlie stood alone in front of the million-dollar case for a long, long time.

13

"MAN, I DON'T KNOW if this is a house or a museum. There's more marble around here than on the Lincoln Memorial."

Jeremy pulled at the oversize paisley tie clipped to the wide collar of his pale blue shirt. The fact that he was twelve and still wearing clip-on ties told Charlie everything he needed to know about Jeremy's knowledge of fashion; instead of a blazer or a suit jacket, he was wearing denim, with dinosaur-emblazoned patches on each elbow. Standing in the center of the marble front foyer of the Caldwell's home, bathed in the orange glow of twin crystal chandeliers hanging from the high arched ceiling, Jeremy put the truth into Anastasia's jibe: Charlie and his friends really did look like they were here to do yard work.

"Over here, guys," Crystal called out. At least she had put on a nice white dress with frilly sleeves and blue buttons running down the back. Of course, she was wearing jeans beneath the dress, and for some reason had chosen high rubber rain boots to complete her look, the very boots she usually wore when trolling streambeds looking for water-polished stones for her collection. "This is really cool."

She'd crossed to the far end of the foyer, where a row of glass display cases took up much of the wall. Charlie reached her side just as Kentaro and Marion entered through the double doors behind him. They'd gotten into an argument on the front porch—something about a Milky Way bar that had gone missing from their hotel room while everyone was getting dressed for the dinner party. Kentaro's denials of having anything to do with the missing candy would have gone over better if his mouth hadn't been covered in chocolate. But they'd obviously reached some sort of détente; Marion's face had returned to its usual pasty-white color, a perfect match to his baggy dress shirt and even baggier beige pants. And Kentaro had wiped most of the chocolate onto the sleeves of his bright red zippered jumpsuit.

"Dude, he really wore this in space. Maybe even in the International Space Station."

The astronaut suit hung in the center case. The suit was mostly white, with dark gaskets at the wrists, neck, and ankles, and patches on both shoulders. An American flag was emblazoned on the right, the NASA logo on the left. Charlie felt chills ride down his spine as he was immediately transported back to the money printing plant, and his conversation with Anastasia. "Conversation" was the wrong word—"threat" was more accurate. He felt his jaw tighten as he shifted his gaze from the astronaut suit to a helmet, in a smaller case to his left. The faceplate was shiny and tinged with gold, so clean he caught his own reflection bugging across the surface. He didn't like what he saw. His jacket and tie—the one nice outfit he'd brought with him from Massachusetts—were fine, but his face looked pale and weak.

What am I doing here? Of course he didn't ask the question out loud; he hadn't yet told his friends about the conversation with Anastasia. It was his fault they were all there. He was the one who had brought them along to the competition. If they were going to get in trouble for faked applications and ruin their chances with NASA, it was going to be because he had trusted Anastasia, a woman he didn't know. It wasn't the first time he'd been fooled like that. He thought back to his entanglement at Incredo Land, and how he had gotten his Whiz Kids involved.

He knew he had to think of a way out. He didn't want to continue to do Anastasia's bidding, but at the moment, he didn't see any other choice. And even though he now doubted she ever even worked for NASA, the task still seemed noble: They were looking for evidence of stolen moon rocks. Even if what they were about to do crossed lines Charlie never intended to cross.

He stepped back from the glass cases and listened to the hum of voices and clinking of glasses coming from the end of the foyer, where the hall opened into a wide banquet area.

"I smell bacon," Marion mumbled, as Charlie led his friends toward the noise. "There's so much pig in the South, isn't there? Pork-belly sliders at the dinner last night, ham sandwiches at the hotel, pigs in blankets coming out of my ears."

"We get it, Marion." Kentaro rolled his eyes. "Clam chowder is the food of the North. Pig is the food of the South. And since this dinner is free, you're about to be in hog heaven."

"Very funny, especially coming from a pipsqueak covered in Milky Way dust."

"I told you: I didn't take your darn candy bar. That's just my toothpaste. It's chocolate flavored—"

"You infants be quiet," Crystal hissed.

They were at edge of the foyer, the dining area unfolding in front of them. It was a huge room with curtained windows, lit by another chandelier. A long table spanned the center of the room—like something from a King Arthur storybook—and white-gloved servers were making the rounds carrying trays loaded with food. The other three teams were already there, though only the kids from Dallas were seated at the table, digging into the dishes in front of them as if they had never seen food before. The team from Worth Hooks was over by a juice bar set up in front of a pair of presidential statues—Washington and Kennedy. They were mingling with Richard Caldwell and two of his team members, both blond, athletic, and tall. Charlie spotted Kelly right next to Caldwell, and he couldn't help noticing how she was looking at the handsome astronaut's son. "With awe" wouldn't have been a bad description. He felt immediately jealous, and then even more guilty for the thought. What right did he have to feel jealous? Caldwell was a nice kid, smart as hell, and truly deserved to be here. Charlie had faked his way in—unknowingly, but still—and was now at Caldwell's house as a spy.

A spy. Well, better a spy than being ousted for perjury. And it wasn't like he was trying to get Richard Caldwell in trouble; it was Caldwell's father who had supposedly taken the moon rocks. Though a man who kept a space suit in his front foyer didn't seem like the type who needed to steal anything.

"So we all know the plan?" Crystal said as they took the first step into the room. "When Charlie gives the signal, we break into two groups. Kentaro, Jeremy, and Marion keep Caldwell and the rest of the room occupied. Charlie and I head for his dad's study, using the map Anastasia left in our hotel room."

Charlie knew that Crystal had already committed the map to memory. The fact that Anastasia had access to a blueprint of Caldwell's house was unnerving—just another stitch of evidence in the mystery of who she really was working for.

"We'll try to move fast," Charlie said. "I don't see any adults in the room, but no doubt they're in the house somewhere. I believe there's a separate cocktail party upstairs for the proctors, with Buzz Caldwell himself."

"You mean we're not going to meet an astronaut tonight?" Jeremy said. "And I got all dressed up for nothing."

He tugged at his clip-on tie again, then headed for the long table, with Kentaro, Crystal, and Marion following close behind. They chose seats across from the Dallas team, Jeremy striking up conversation as the servers swarmed over with pitcher after pitcher of water.

Charlie found himself drawn in a different direction. He reached the group by the juice bar just as Richard Caldwell was finishing what must have been an epic story, judging from the expressions on his audience's faces. Even Ryan's big mouth was sufficiently slack, his eyes wide beneath his Neanderthal brow.

"And that's where we came down," Caldwell was saying. "Right on the White House's front lawn. Both helicopter engines burned out, smoke coming out of the tail. We must have spun around twenty times. My father barely got control of the thing, by using an old trick he'd picked up in the air force to stabilize the chopper. He'd pulled on the cyclic stick—it's the lever that controls a chopper—in exactly the right sequence to get it to stop spinning. Left, left, right, left, right, right. Nobody got hurt. Not my dad, not me, not the vice president. But you can bet they left the test flying of experimental choppers to the experts after that, believe me!"

As the Worth Hooks kids clapped in amazement,

and Caldwell's own two team members turned to order matching grapefruit juices from the bar, Caldwell saw Charlie edging in from the back of the group and greeted him with a wide smile.

"Sorry to be grandstanding over here—welcome, Charlie! Glad you could make it. You missed my dad's speech. He was in here for a whole five minutes—a new record, I think. Now he's upstairs with the proctors and some VIPs from his aerospace company. Any excuse to talk business. So we have the place to ourselves."

"Ain't no party like an astronaut party," Ryan butted in. "First person to put on the suit and spacewalk across the Jell-O mold wins a moon rock!"

Kelly looked at him like she wanted to slap the grin off his face. Then she gave Charlie a hug, surprising and embarrassing him at the same time.

"Nice showing today. Didn't have a chance to congratulate you earlier; you guys ran off with your proctor almost as soon as you won. Your plane was amazing."

Charlie shrugged, smelling her perfume in the air. He imagined those floral particles clinging to his shirt sleeves, and wondered how long he could wait to wash the thing when he got home to Massachusetts.

"Even a stopped clock gets it right a couple times a

day," he said. "Hopefully we don't embarrass ourselves in the semifinals."

"Oh, you'll be embarrassed," Ryan said. "They announced the lineup before you got here. You'll be playing us to see who ends up in the finals against Richie, here."

"Hey," Caldwell said. "We still have to beat the team from Dallas."

"That glass of grapefruit juice could beat the team from Dallas. Come to think of it, even Charlie here could probably beat the team from Dallas. They're only this far because they got here on a lucky throw. Too bad he's got to go up against us," Ryan bellowed.

Kelly gave Ryan a shove. He stuck his tongue out at her, then led the rest of the Worth Hooks team away toward the long dinner table.

"I feel like I'm constantly apologizing for him," she said. The words were meant for Charlie, but she kept looking at Richard.

Charlie felt the familiar tinge of jealousy again but pushed it away. "I'm sure we'll all do our best," he managed. He couldn't have sounded more lame.

Caldwell laughed and clapped him on the shoulder. "We'll all be working extra hard to keep up with you.

And now that I know about your secret weapon, I'm going to be up all night retooling our plane."

Charlie looked at him. He could feel Kelly's gaze ping-ponging between the two boys. "Our secret weapon?"

"My dad told me about your proctor. Anastasia Federov. He hadn't noticed her name on the application sheet at first. Turns out they used to work together."

"At NASA?" Charlie asked.

"No, this was after they both left NASA. Anastasia was hired by a small start-up aeronautics firm outside DC, just about the same time my father helped found AI. They're competitors now."

Charlie's throat felt constricted. Anastasia worked for a rival aeronautics firm. And he was in Caldwell's house, as a spy. They had a term for this. *Corporate espionage.* Charlie was pretty sure it was illegal. Maybe even worse than lying on an application form.

"My dad says you're in good hands," Caldwell continued. "She's supposed to be one heck of a flight engineer. Really great scientist, despite what happened with her at NASA."

"What happened at NASA?" Kelly asked, saving Charlie the trouble.

"She left after some sort of disagreement with the

director of her lab. They were working on new materials for spacecraft—the same thing my dad works on now—and they were on the verge of a breakthrough involving a new type of metal. Anastasia thought it was something that could make a lot of money for the right company, but her boss felt it should remain a NASA development. So she left the company and joined the start-up. Rumor is, she's still working on the same material. But she hasn't gotten anywhere yet. I guess her research has stalled enough to give her time to proctor and advise your paper airplane team. Good news for you!"

Charlie was trying to take in everything Caldwell had said when he saw Crystal making eyes at him from the dinner table. The noise level in the room was at its peak, and the Worth Hooks team—minus Kelly—was at the table as well. This was as good a moment as they were going to get. Charlie would have to digest the information about Anastasia later. For the moment, he needed to return to his role as a reluctant spy.

He ran a hand through his hair, and Crystal nodded. Then she made the same motion, hand through her hair, toward Jeremy, Kentaro, and Marion. Jeremy and Marion nodded, but Kentaro was so deep into a bowl of pork stew he didn't notice until Jeremy picked up a dinner roll and lofted it at Kentaro's forehead, hitting him right between the eyes.

Kentaro looked up, then nodded. And then he climbed up onto his chair, standing up to his full height.

"Ladies and gents, I'd like to make a toast. To our host with the most, the only kid I've ever met who can bring a space suit to show-and-tell. Richard, how about a few words to get this night going right?"

The sight of Kentaro in his bright red jump-suit standing on a chair had the crowd smiling, and Caldwell couldn't have resisted, even if he'd wanted to. He excused himself from Charlie and Kelly and headed toward the table. Kelly gave Charlie's hand a squeeze, then followed.

"Maybe just one story," Caldwell started, and Charlie knew he had his moment.

14

"SLOW DOWN, TIGER. YOU'RE going to get us noticed."

Crystal was breathing hard behind Charlie as she struggled to keep up with his pace. His socks were moving so fast against the thick Oriental carpet that ran down the center of the long hallway leading into the interior of the home that he actually thought he might see sparks. It had been Crystal's idea to ditch their shoes in the planter next to the steps that had led down from the dining level to their target area on Anastasia's map to make their journey more soundless, but she somehow seemed to move slower without those rubber soles. Or maybe it was just the adrenaline coursing through Charlie's veins, pushing him to get this over with as fast as he could.

"The faster we go, the less chance we have of anybody spotting us down here."

"Yeah, but if we do get caught, we're going to look mighty suspicious jogging through the house at top speed. Don't forget our cover story: We got turned around looking for the bathroom."

It had to be the oldest cover story in the book, but Charlie hadn't had time to come up with anything better.

"Sometimes you need to run when you're looking for the bathroom. Maybe we don't do so well with a menu consisting of eighty different variations of pork."

"You're disgusting," Crystal said. "Better not let your new girlfriend hear you talk like that. She's going to run for the hills."

Charlie slowed enough to toss a look at Crystal over his shoulder. "She's not my girlfriend. She's just nice, that's all."

"Nice girls don't hang around with bullies like Ryan."

"Ryan's a special case. He's had a rough life. They've all had it pretty rough, and they don't have a lot of the things we have."

"Cry me a river," Crystal said. "Why are you making excuses for her anyways? Ryan isn't her charity case; he's her teammate and friend."

Charlie thought he detected more than a hint of jealousy in Crystal's voice.

"You're as pretty as she is," Charlie tried. "You just make different choices about how you present yourselves."

Crystal stopped dead in her tracks and put her hands on her hips.

"Charlie, for a smart kid you really are an idiot."

Charlie stopped too, looking at her. He had no idea what he'd said wrong, or why she was suddenly so mad. He'd never really understood girls. And the truth was, he'd never really thought of Crystal as a *girl*. Not in that way. But he had noticed, she did tend to get angry whenever he paid attention to other girls like Kelly. He chalked it up to a bit of possessiveness; the Whiz Kids were a close bunch, after all. It couldn't be anything personal. This was Crystal.

"Look, Kelly seems to have eyes for only one kid in this competition, and we're sneaking around his house. Something we better get back to quickly, before someone notices we're gone."

"We don't need to sneak any farther," Crystal huffed, pointing ahead.

Right in front of them was a thick wooden door with an electronic keypad to one side.

"This is going to be tricky," Charlie said, happy to be changing the subject.

He tried the door, confirming that it was locked. Then he approached the keypad. There were fifty numbered keys spread across the face of the rectangular device and space for a five-number code. Charlie quickly did the math. Fifty keys, a five-number combo—that worked out to 254,251,200 possible permutations. *Two hundred and fifty-four million . . .*

"Move out of my way, lover boy."

Crystal gave him a little shove, then stepped in front of the electronic lock. She reached into the pocket of her dress and removed a glass test tube filled with yellowish-tan powder.

"What the heck is that?" Charlie asked.

She carefully opened the top of the test tube.

"Just a little something from my travel collection."

Crystal hadn't let any of the other Whiz Kids sift through the small tackle box she kept in her suitcase, and they'd assumed it contained her favorite rocks, the ones she couldn't bear to leave at home, even for a week-long trip. Obviously, it contained more than just some polished quartz.

"It's called lycopodium powder. It's derived from a species of moss called *Lycopodium clavatum*. Wolf's foot, as it's more commonly known. You might want to step back, because it's actually quite flammable when it touches air. They use it in fireworks and explosives."

Charlie nearly jumped to the other side of the hallway.

"You're going to blow the door up?"

"No, even though it's flammable, it's so light that in small quantities, it burns right up in the air. Magicians use it to create bright flashes to distract their audiences. But it also has another property. It's used to dust for fingerprints. See, the human finger contains an inordinate amount of oils. When you touch something, like a key on an electronic lock, you leave some of these oils behind. Certain powders can detect these oils."

She carefully leaned toward the keypad and tipped the test tube, spilling just the tiniest amount of powder over the keys. Most of the powder burned in the air before it hit the ground, but almost immediately, five of the keys caught a light dusting of the yellowish-tan stuff.

"There you go. Zero, two, seven, six, nine."

Charlie whistled.

"That was amazing—but wait. If these are the right numbers, what order do they go in?"

"The powder can't tell us that," Crystal said, capping the test tube and putting it back in her pocket. "But maybe we can figure it out."

Five numbers still left 120 possible combinations. It would take them a long time to try them all out, and there was a very good chance the lock would have some sort of safety mechanism that set off an alarm if they tried more than three.

They had to figure it out another way. Five numbers, one combination. Zero, two, seven, six, nine. Charlie closed his eyes and let the numbers bounce around inside his head. *Zero, two, seven, six, nine.* He realized there was something familiar about those numbers, something that his subconscious recognized, even though his conscious mind couldn't quite see it.

"Maybe we should turn back," Crystal said. "Tell Anastasia we have to find another time to sneak in. If we had a black light, we might be able to see which keys had more finger oil than the rest, and make a better guess as to which was pressed later than the rest."

"We don't need a black light," Charlie said suddenly.

And then he opened his eyes.

He moved straight to the keypad and began hitting numbers.

"Seven. Two. Zero. Six. Nine."

There was a loud metallic click, and the door swung inward.

"How did you do that?"

Charlie grinned.

"Numbers is my name, isn't it?"

"Charlie."

"Seven. Twenty. Sixty-nine. It's the date of the first moon landing. What better password is there for a former astronaut?"

With that, he led her through the open doorway.

15

IF THEY HAD THOUGHT the foyer looked like a museum, with its marble floors, elegant chandeliers, and the astronaut suit, Buzz Caldwell's "study" was even more grand. Here the floors were carpeted, and the ceilings lit by ornate sconces jutting from the even more ornate molding—but every square inch of wall was covered by display cases containing space paraphernalia that would rival any collection of the Smithsonian's. The front of the room contained three glass cases with mahogany trim, all of them tall enough to come up way past Charlie's head. Inside each case stood an astronaut space suit, but these weren't the white "indoor" suits like the one in the foyer, these were bright orange and excessively bulky, with helmets embossed in gold as big as a giant bug's eye. Charlie knew from his own reading that the orange color hadn't been chosen as a fashion statement; orange, it turned out, offered the biggest contrast to ocean water. These suits had been designed for ocean rescue, after the astronaut completed his guided plummet back to Earth.

"'Advanced Crew Escape Suit,'" Crystal whispered, reading the words from a metal plate at the base of the display case. "Can you imagine zooming down from space in one of those? I mean, you're inside a capsule, but still. You couldn't get me inside one of those for fifty cash prizes."

Charlie felt differently; heck, he'd have traded college to go to space. But Crystal was a rock hound, so it was no surprise she intended to keep her feet on solid earth.

"The suits are more than just protection," Charlie said. "They contain air, water, medical supplies, and a parachute. If there's an accident on the way down, the astronaut can jettison himself and come down in just the suit. Pretty insane."

Charlie felt a new pang of guilt. Buzz Caldwell had actually been in one of these suits, and now Charlie was sneaking around his study. He pushed the thought away as he saw Crystal move to a new set of display cases. Her eyes went wide. It was like she'd just found the Hope Diamond.

"Rock samples," she whispered.

Charlie rushed to her side. *Will it possibly be this easy?*

But when he got next to her, he realized she wasn't looking at moon rocks. Anyone else would have had trouble identifying the three-centimeter-long, egg-shaped, black-and-gray-speckled sample, but Crystal knew what it was immediately.

"A meteorite. That one too—" She pointed to a rusty-orange rock next to the egg-shaped one. "That was found in Arizona; it's mostly iron. Highly magnetic. And next to that, a ten-centimeter meteorite from Africa. Look at the large surface dimples and the rich black crust. You only see that in newly fallen meteorites. They get that way because they are superheated on their way down through the atmosphere. Geez, this is like a space-rock candy shop!"

Charlie was happy for her enthusiasm, but he concentrated on searching for moon rock clues. There were obviously no moon rocks in the case, but toward the back, he did see something inside the glass that made him pause. An old metallic-looking case, unlocked and open. Within the case were a half dozen pale yellow velvet grooves, big enough to have once contained fairly large rock samples.

"I can't be sure, but I think that might have been

where they were once stored," Charlie said. "That case looks old—maybe dating back to the sixties or seventies. It could very well have come from NASA. Anastasia would probably know for sure. Do you have your camera?"

"You think I carry a test tube full of fingerprint powder, but I don't have a camera?"

She reached into her other dress pocket and retrieved Kentaro's disposable camera. She held it up to the case and flicked the switch. To both their surprises, the flash went off, temporarily blinding them in the fairly dark room.

"You didn't turn off the flash?!" Charlie hissed.

"Wouldn't have been able to see anything in the picture!"

"Yeah, but that was bright. If someone was walking by—"

Charlie stopped talking as a strange metallic clicking filled the air. He turned his head up, toward the source of the noise, and saw a mounted camera in the far corner of the room tracking toward them.

"A security camera," he hissed. "It wasn't activated when we came in, because we used the proper security code on the lock. But the flash must have set it off."

"Let's move. We can get past if we stay low."

Charlie hoped she was right. He dropped to a crawl

and skittered as fast as he could toward the door. Crystal was so close she was nearly grabbing at his socks. A moment later, they were almost into the hall when Crystal tapped his ankle. He looked back and saw that she was pointing to a group of magnetic ID cards hanging from a hook on the wall, right by the door.

"Aerospace Infinity key cards," she whispered. "They might come in handy."

"We need to get out of here—"

"I can reach one," Crystal said. Before Charlie could stop her, she leaped up, swiping the top card from the hook. Then she was back into her crawl.

A second later, they were out into the carpeted hallway, breathing hard.

"That was dangerous," Charlie coughed. "If the camera had caught us . . ."

He left the thought hanging in the air. Crystal shrugged, holding the ID card up in front of her. Then she turned it over and paused.

"Look, Charlie. Is this what I think it is?"

It took Charlie a moment to understand the perspective, but then his eyes widened.

"A map," he said. "I think it's the Air and Space Museum. That section over there is the track where we had our competition, where we'll have the semis and finals tomorrow. But what is that green dot? An exhibit of some sort?"

"These cards don't open exhibits, Charlie. These open doorways. I think we just found a way into Aerospace Infinity's laboratories."

Charlie stared at her, stunned.

"You think Aerospace Infinity has a lab inside the Air and Space Museum?"

"Not *inside.*"

"Then where?"

Crystal stuffed the ID card into her pocket, next to the test tube. She wasn't going to tell him any more here. Even so, Charlie had to admit, she made a darn good spy. James Bond had nothing on Crystal Mueller.

"Let's get back to the party," she said, rising to her feet as the study door clicked shut behind them. "By now, knowing Kentaro, Caldwell has been forced to tell enough stories to get everyone to the moon and back ten times over."

Charlie followed her back down the hall, stifling the urge to jog as they worked their way back toward the dining floor. On the outside, they tried to look as casual as possible, but neither of them stopped breathing hard until the scent of bacon once again hovered in the air.

16

"WELL, THIS IS A first! We have a tie!"

The referee's voice reverberated through the overhead speaker system as the crowd erupted in noise. The entire hall seemed to tremble with the sound, and Charlie felt himself instinctively shrinking back at the starting line, his eyes still focused on the little fleck of white so far down the track it looked like a drop of snow.

A hundred and eighty-nine feet, another new record—except this time, Charlie's plane wasn't sitting on the record-breaking finish mark alone. Right next to his tiny fleck of white sat another snowflake. The two airplanes had landed at exactly the same spot, their noses right next to each other. So close that the referee had resorted to a ruler to confirm—a tie.

"I really didn't think you had it in you."

Ryan was standing next to Charlie on the starting line, and he, too, seemed to have shrunk back a step in the face of all that noise. Charlie looked at him, surprised.

"No snarky remark? No joke about my weak arm or bad eyesight?"

Ryan grinned.

"Not today, shrimp. That was a real good throw. I thought my pitch was unbeatable. Well, technically, it was. But maybe Kelly isn't entirely wrong about you."

Despite the moment, despite all the noise and the pressure, Charlie couldn't help himself.

"Kelly said something about me?"

Ryan rolled his eyes. Then he turned around and jogged through the applauding crowd back to his folding table. He was right—there was no time to talk; they were both going to need a second plane to break the tie. The winner was going against Caldwell in the finals. Caldwell's plane, which had dispatched the plane from the Dallas team by a good twenty feet, at a totally respectable 180 feet, was as sleek and perfect as ever. Charlie and Ryan had both just set a record, beating Caldwell's distance, but every throw was different. A

breath of wind, a patch of humid air, a bit of dust—
anything could shake up a throw at those distances.

Charlie headed to his own folding table. As he went,
he cast another look toward the referee's table, where
the ref was still at the microphone, telling the competitors they would have three minutes to make a new plane.
Next to the ref, Charlie could still see the three men
he'd noticed earlier, when he'd first gotten to the starting line. All three were carrying notebooks and wearing
matching flight jackets. The NASA emblem was impossible to miss, emblazoned on each of the jackets' right
shoulder. NASA had sent officials to witness the finals,
and no doubt they were taking notes on the competitors. Charlie had to assume his name was now near the
top of whatever lists they might be making.

Exciting—and terrifying. He wondered how quickly
they'd tear out that page if they knew what he was really
doing in the competition, or how he'd gotten there. He
pushed the thought away as he reached his team's folding table.

"Almost done," Kentaro said, as his fingers moved
rapidly, creasing edges and double-folding flaps on a
piece of pristine white paper. "I'm going to add the tiniest bit of weight to the nose. I think we can get another
few inches, if the throw is just right."

Marion had his sketchbook open to their design, his stubby finger tracing the edges of his drawing as he watched Kentaro fold. Jeremy looked like he was about to pass out, his gangly arms wrapped around his body to keep him upright. Crystal was the only one who didn't look worried. In fact, she looked *confident.*

"Charlie," she said, quietly. "I want you to make a slight adjustment to your throw. Instead of thirty-six degrees, try for thirty-three."

"Isn't that too low?"

She raised a hand, feeling the air.

"It's five degrees cooler today than yesterday. That means the higher air is going to be a little less dense. A lower flight will be a longer flight. Trust me."

If Charlie was going to trust anyone today, it was going to be Crystal.

Finally, Kentaro made the last fold and held the plane up in front of the team.

"It's beautiful," Charlie managed.

Kentaro grinned.

"I really think I'm getting the hang of this. Maybe I should go into business. Kentaro Mori's Paper Plane Emporium. We could sell them down by the train station."

Charlie took the plane from his hand just as a loud buzzer went off across the hall. It was time.

Charlie jogged back through the crowd to the starting line. He reached it just as Ryan arrived, Kelly at his side. Charlie watched as Kelly handed Ryan their plane—still a flying fox design, but with a more tapered tail. Kelly gave Ryan's arm a squeeze, then looked right at Charlie.

"Good luck," she said. "If someone's got to beat us, I'm glad it might be you."

Charlie blushed. Ryan groaned.

"Yeah, I'd be thrilled to be beaten by a runt with a plane made by a hobbit."

Back to the old Ryan. The ref came over next to them, a coin in his hand. As he flipped it, he nodded to Charlie to make the call.

"Heads," Charlie cried.

The whole room seemed to suck into itself as the coin spun in the air. When it landed tails, Charlie grimaced to himself. That meant he'd be throwing first. It was always an advantage to throw second. Ryan and Kelly both stepped back, giving Charlie room. It felt like every eye in the place was on him. Sweat beaded on the back of his neck, but he tried to close his mind off, to focus on the plane, the track, and the numbers.

Thirty-three degrees. He could see the angle like it was drawn right in the air. He took a deep breath, cocked his arm—and threw.

The only sound in the room was shaped paper cutting through air. Charlie's plane rose ten feet toward the ceiling, then began to level off. It's flight was slow, like before, but even steadier—as if the extra folds Kentaro had added had adjusted the material of the nose just enough to counter the difference in air density from the day before. The plane was simply sailing, as if it were never going to come down.

"Unbelievable."

The whisper came from Charlie's left, and he glanced over to see Richard Caldwell standing by the sideline. Richard was watching the plane, and the look on his face was nearly ecstatic. To Richard, this wasn't about the competition, it was about the planes themselves. Richard was a true scientist. Charlie had to believe that such a kid couldn't have come from a bad father. Richard had mentioned again and again that his father was hard on him, but Charlie couldn't believe that the man was a thief.

Charlie turned his gaze back to his plane and was shocked to see that it was still sailing forward. It wasn't until another ten seconds passed that the nose started to dip downward. And then it descended, gradually, softly, slowly. Finally, it touched down.

"One hundred and ninety!"

Charlie gasped. He couldn't believe that something he'd thrown had gone that far. As Ryan stepped forward to take his place at the starting line, he could see the fear in the bigger kid's eyes. The confidence was gone, the bluster evaporated.

"Good luck," Charlie said.

Ryan didn't answer. Instead, he cocked his muscled arm as far back as he could and let it fly.

His fox tore into the air at an incredible speed, cutting an upward arc toward the ceiling. Twice as high as Charlie's plane, and more than twice as fast. The crowd made a sound somewhere between a gasp and a cheer. Nobody had seen a plane go that fast. Higher and higher—faster and faster—and then, something began to happen.

The plane began to slow. As Crystal had predicted, the higher air was slightly less dense—and that density was causing drag against the fox ears and tail. The plane began to tremble, and then it was going downward, finishing the second half of the parabola.

"No," Ryan mouthed. "No, no, no."

Charlie felt his pain. Ryan's mouth curved downward, and his shoulders slumped. Charlie wanted to say something to make the kid feel better. Even though he had a mean streak a mile wide, it was obvious this competition was truly important to him. If what Kelly had said was true, Ryan needed to win if he was going to afford college one day. Charlie *wanted* to win. But Ryan *needed* to win.

But even needs couldn't trump math, and in the end, this was a contest of numbers. Ryan's numbers didn't add up. The four forces were out of balance. His plane descended lower, lower, then tipped forward, plunging straight to the ground.

"A hundred and eighty-eight."

Another great throw, but not far enough. The crowd erupted again. Charlie turned to shake Ryan's hand, but the kid was already slumping back toward his team. Charlie saw Kelly putting her arm on his shoulder. Then she caught Charlie's gaze.

"Congrats," she said.

Then she looked toward Richard, who was stepping forward, his perfectly symmetrical plane in hand. She turned back toward Charlie.

"Win, Charlie. You deserve it."

Charlie felt his face blanch. He couldn't believe she wanted him to beat Caldwell. He was still staring at her as Caldwell took his position next to him. Kentaro, Marion, Jeremy, and Crystal had arrived as well, all of them jumping up and down. Kentaro had a new plane in his hand, ready to go. It looked even better than the previous planes. The referee approached, that fate-deciding coin in hand.

"You pick," Caldwell said, still clearly impressed. "You've earned it."

Charlie shook his head. Part of him wanted nothing more than to fulfill Kelly's request—to beat Richard Caldwell, to beat the best and prove himself truly worthwhile. But Kelly and Richard were both wrong. Charlie didn't deserve anything. And he still had work to do.

He stepped back, then pulled Kentaro forward to the starting line.

"Actually, I'm not going to be throwing this time. Our lead designer is taking my place."

Kentaro looked smaller and more terrified than ever as he took his place next to Richard at the line. The referee shrugged, then flipped the coin.

"Call it!" he shouted.

"Tails!" Kentaro managed, his voice a squeak above the crowd.

And heads it was. The crowd roared as Richard stepped back, leaving Kentaro alone on the line.

Charlie knew what Kentaro was feeling—the mixture of fear and excitement and pride, the tenseness flowing through his muscles, and the daggers stabbing at the pit of his stomach. He wished he could stand there and watch, he wished he could be there for support, but instead, he slipped backward through the crowd. And just as he had predicted, nobody noticed, not even Kelly. They were too busy watching the final two competitors. Too busy waiting for those final two throws.

Charlie didn't stop moving until he was out the door and in the hallway that led into the rest of the museum. A second later, Crystal exited after him, already pulling the key card out of her pocket.

"That was amazing," she said. "And it worked perfectly. Nobody is going to notice that we're gone until the contest is over. Jeremy and Marion will look out for Caldwell's dad and keep tabs on Anastasia. So for now, it's just you and me."

She grabbed his hand and led him down the hall, the key card out in front of her. She was reading the map off the back of the plastic, taking them toward the bright green dot. To Charlie's surprise, once they had matched their location to the perspective of the tiny map, they didn't have far to go. Down the hall, one turn, and they were inside the room with the gigantic nose of the Boeing 747. They passed through a smattering of tourists, then under the shadow of the curved half an aircraft. Charlie fought the urge to look up to see his reflection traipse across the smooth fuselage as he followed Crystal to the far corner of the room.

In front of them was a huge Boeing jet engine, nearly the size of a pickup truck. The engine was cylindrical, shaped vaguely like a stubby rocket, a swirling fan covering its cavernous front, and its tail tapering off to a near point. Crystal stopped in front of the engine, looking closely at the card.

"This doesn't make sense," Charlie said, looking over her shoulder. "The green dot is right here."

Crystal lowered the card, and then pointed toward the floor. Charlie saw that the engine was up on a legged pedestal; there was about a foot of space beneath the massive machine and the carpeted floor.

"What?"

"Look closer."

Charlie squinted and saw a discolored square of carpet, right beneath the engine's tail. He checked behind himself, making sure none of the other tourists were looking, and then bent down on one knee.

The square of carpet came up without much effort. Underneath was an electronic keypad, similar to the one outside Buzz Caldwell's study.

"See, I told you Aeronautics Infinity didn't have a

lab inside the Air and Space Museum," Crystal said.

"It has one underneath," Charlie finished for her.

Crystal handed him the key card, and he swiped it through a slot above the keypad. There was a quiet whirr, and a section of the carpet beneath the engine whiffed open, revealing metal stairs leading downward.

17

"CHROME. I SEE A lot of chrome. Somebody better be getting paid a pretty penny to do all the polishing, because this place sparkles like the Fourth of July."

Crystal was only two steps ahead of him as they descended the stairs into the underground lab, but she'd already managed to find a light switch, bathing the thousand-square-foot cube of a room in bright fluorescent light. And she was right. Now Charlie could see the chrome, flashing up at him from nearly every angle.

The lab was state-of-the-art, much nicer than anything he'd ever seen while visiting his dad and mom at MIT. Aside from the chrome—shelves, glass cabinets, sinks, test-tube racks—the place was mostly a cinder-block cube, filled with sophisticated devices and workstations. Charlie was able to pick out autoclaves and centrifuges, test tubes, and enough beakers to build a mini glass metropolis; Charlie also recognized a pair of giant electron microscopes by the far wall.

But what dominated his thoughts as he reached the bottom step, right behind Crystal, was a huge object he saw in the corner to his left, between two of the sink stations. Crystal saw it too, letting out a low whistle.

"Now *that's* a safe."

It was a humongous monstrosity of a safe. Six feet tall, with a thick metal door that looked to be iron or steel. Right in the center of the door was a single wheel—a simple locking mechanism, no buttons or keys. Anachronistic, maybe, in this place of electronics and engines, but to Charlie, it made perfect sense. Electronics could be beaten by intelligence and math; he and Crystal had already proven that fact back at Caldwell's house. Old-fashioned iron and steel didn't care how smart you were or what tricks you had up your sleeve.

Charlie had a sinking feeling in his stomach as he followed Crystal across the lime-green tiles that covered the floor. He felt certain that what they were looking for had to be in that safe, but he couldn't imagine how they were going to get inside.

As they got closer he focused on the big wheel in the center of the door. It wasn't chrome, but it still shone like the cabinets and sinks, bathed in the fluorescent light. Even from a distance, he could see how the wheel worked. It could spin clockwise or counterclockwise. To open the door, you had to know the precise directions to spin it: which way, and how many times each way. Unlike the numbered electronic lock, the possibilities were impossible to calculate—the number of turns each way had no limits, no numerical parameters.

As Crystal came to a stop in front of the wheel, she reached out and touched the heavy metal of the door.

"This has to be a foot thick. There's no way to cut or burn our way in, even if we had the materials. I could try the lycopodium powder. We could see where the wheel was touched."

"That isn't going to help," Charlie said. "You have to turn it in the proper sequence. Left, right, left, whatever."

"Like a steering wheel," Crystal said, crestfallen. "Then it's finished, Charlie. We can't get through."

Charlie paused, as what she said pricked at his thoughts. *Like a steering wheel.*

"Or a cyclic stick," he whispered.

Crystal looked at him.

Charlie stepped forward and put his hands on the

wheel. The metal felt cold against his palms. He thought back to the dinner party and the tail end of the story he'd heard Richard Caldwell telling Kelly and Ryan. Charlie had mostly been focused on Kelly at the time, but he could still remember Caldwell's words. *My father barely got control of the thing, by using an old trick he'd picked up in the air force to stabilize the chopper. . . .*

Left. Left. Right. Left. Right. Right.

Charlie turned the wheel as the sequence ran through his head. The wheel creaked with each motion. Left, left, right, left, right, right—

Bang. There was the sound of an iron tumbler falling free, and suddenly the huge door was swinging outward. Charlie jumped back, nearly knocking Crystal over as they both got out of the way. The next thing they knew, they were facing an open vault, about four feet deep. The vault was lined with shelves. Charlie took a step forward, quickly looking through the shelves, and then his gaze rested on a row of three vials near the center of the vault.

"Moon rocks," Charlie said quietly. Then he paused.

Two of the vials contained the same gray, pock-marked stones that Anastasia had shown him back at the Nagassack lunchroom. But the third vial appeared to have an entirely different substance in it. Even compared to all the chrome in the lab, the flecked material inside the vial sparkled like trapped fireflies. Instead of being stone shaped, the material was long and flat, not something that had been found—something that had been *manufactured*.

"What is that?" Charlie said.

Crystal reached forward and carefully took the third vial out of the vault. She looked at it closely, then gave it a shake. Charlie waited for her response. She was, after all, an expert, perhaps as qualified as any university professor.

"I think I saw something over here that might help," she said, stepping back from the safe and heading toward one of the nearby cabinets.

"You're not going to try and run it through an electron microscope, are you? We don't have time for that."

"Don't be foolish. I'm going to do something much simpler. Here we go."

She grabbed a small black object, about the size of stapler, out of the cabinet. Then she held the object right up against the glass of the vial.

There was a click as the shiny specimen moved against the glass, the sparkling flecks on the material standing on end like little hairs.

"Magnetic," she said, showing Charlie that the

stapler-shaped object in her hands was, indeed, a magnet. "This material is manufactured metal, with magnetic properties. I can see that it's incredibly smooth yet probably pliable. And it's not made out of any materials that metal has been made out of before."

"Then what's it made out of?" Charlie asked.

Crystal pointed to the two other vials still on the shelf in the vault.

"Moon rocks."

Charlie blinked. So that's what this was about. Not just stolen moon rocks, a new metal made out of stolen moon rocks. His mind began putting the pieces together. Anastasia had left NASA because she had wanted to profit from the development of new aerospace metals. She now worked for a competing aerospace company. She wasn't after the moon rocks, she was after the metal Buzz Caldwell and his firm had synthesized from the rocks.

That still didn't explain what the rocks were doing here, or whether Caldwell had stolen them from NASA. But it solidified the fact that what Charlie and his friends were engaged in was corporate espionage of the highest order.

He couldn't let Anastasia have this metal, or these rocks. But he couldn't just leave them here and try to go to the police, or NASA. It would still be his word against hers. He needed real, solid evidence. He needed to see this through.

He reached out and grabbed the two vials full of moon rocks, then took the vial of the new metal from Crystal. He put all three into his backpack.

"We've got to move," he said. "If we're lucky, we can get these to the proper authorities, and they can sort it all out."

Crystal nodded. Together, they rushed back to the stairs leading into the museum. Charlie took the stairs two at a time, Crystal nearly bumping into his heels. He was careful as he reached the top, pulling himself out of the opening with his head bowed low so as not to bump against the bottom of the Boeing 747 engine. Then he turned around to help Crystal after him.

It wasn't until they'd crawled out from under the engine, the slab of carpet sliding shut behind them, that Charlie realized they weren't alone.

High leather boots. Black leggings. A gray sheath dress. Wide, reflective sunglasses.

Anastasia was standing in front of them, a smile on her thin lips. Porter was next to her, his crew cut as sharp and close as ever. A second man was behind Porter, with a similar crew cut, and even more muscles bulging beneath his tight black T-shirt. Anastasia stepped forward, holding out a manicured hand.

"Hello, Charlie," she said through her tight grin. "I think you have something for me. The sooner you hand it over, the sooner we can put all of this behind us."

Charlie involuntarily stepped back, nearly knocking Crystal into the jet engine.

"Charlie," Anastasia said, "we can do this the easy way."

She smiled even wider, gesturing to Porter, who had taken a step forward.

"Or we can do this Mr. Porter's way."

18

CHARLIE FELT HIS ENTIRE body begin to tremble. He could feel the weight of his backpack against his shoulder. He knew he had no choice. Porter was huge, the man behind him even bigger—but he didn't want to hand over the backpack. He looked past Anastasia. The closest tourists were a good ten yards away. Nobody was near enough to see what was going on, and everyone's attention was pinned to that 747, which took up most of the room.

"You tricked us," Charlie said, playing for time. "You don't care about the moon rocks. You wanted the new metal."

"They aren't mutually exclusive. As I'm sure you've guessed, the metal is made from the moon rocks themselves. It's going to be the key to building super-light airplanes and rockets, which will fly better and faster. And I wasn't lying, Charlie. Hand it over without any fuss, and I'll make sure you all get recommendations to NASA. This can be good for all of us."

"But mostly good for you," Crystal said. Charlie noticed that her left hand had fallen down next to her side. Her fingers were inching toward her pocket. She was up to something, but he wasn't sure what. "This isn't about NASA. This is about money. Caldwell's company used the rocks to make the metal, and now you want to steal it and reverse engineer it, then sell it yourself. You're a liar and a thief."

Anastasia sighed.

"You kids have a lot to learn. This isn't thievery—it's business. The American way."

She turned toward Porter. "Mr. Porter, I think we have to do this your way," she started, when there was a shout from behind her.

Charlie looked to see Kentaro, Marion, and Jeremy running toward them. Kentaro was in front, a huge smile on his face.

"Charlie, you're not going to believe what happened! The plane—"

Kentaro stopped midsentence, skidding on his heels

as he saw Anastasia and her thugs. Jeremy and Marion nearly crashed into him from behind.

A moment of worry crossed Anastasia's face, but she quickly turned back toward Charlie.

"Porter," she shouted. "Get the backpack, now!"

Porter started forward, and suddenly Crystal yanked something out of her pocket and threw it toward the floor. Charlie had less than a second to realize what it was. There was a sudden flash of bright light as the powder ignited, sparked by the kinetic energy of the breaking glass, and a huge orange flame leaped four feet into the air when the test tube full of lycopodium powder shattered against the ground.

Anastasia fell backward, crashing into Porter. Porter and the other thug shielded their eyes, screaming like little kids. Charlie and Crystal leaped forward, dodging the flame, even as it burned itself out and disappeared in a puff of black smoke.

"Scatter!" Charlie yelled.

Crystal ran to the left, Jeremy and Marion toward the other side of the room. Charlie ran straight ahead, almost colliding with Kentaro. There was a brief moment as they tangled together and then quickly separated. Kentaro gave Charlie a strange look, but Charlie didn't have time to contemplate what it meant. He hit the ground running, his legs moving as fast they could. He headed right through the crowd looking at the 747 nose, then burst through the door back into the hallway that led to the rest of museum. As he turned the first corner, he thought he might have just made it. Then he looked back, and his stomach dropped. Porter and the other crew cut crashed out through the doorway and into the hallway behind him, not ten feet behind.

Charlie screamed inwardly and rocketed forward, heading straight for the main atrium.

He couldn't let Porter catch him. He needed to get those vials to the authorities—the police, NASA, whoever. He had to lose Porter and the other man somehow, but they were big and fast, and the looks on their faces emanated pure anger.

Charlie reached the edge of the main atrium. The place was twice as crowded as the first time he'd gone through it—the sea of tourists around the Apollo capsule had to be ten thick—and Charlie knew he wasn't going to get very far going straight through. Instead, he cut to his left and found himself in front of a stairwell leading up to the second-floor exhibits. Without a thought, he dove right on through—

"Charlie? You look like you've seen a ghost!"

Charlie nearly ran headlong into Richard Caldwell,

coming down from upstairs. Charlie skidded to a stop. He knew he only had a few seconds until Porter figured out where he'd gone, and he had to make them count.

"Richard, there's something I need to tell you—"

"And there's something I need to tell you, man. Congratulations! What an amazing win. Your boy Kentaro broke the Guinness World Record. I don't know how he did it, but he got that plane of yours to go two hundred and thirty feet! It nearly hit the back wall of the hall—"

"Richard, listen to me!" Charlie didn't have time to think about the amazing feat Kentaro had pulled off. "I've uncovered something about your father. His aerospace company is using stolen moon rocks to make a special metal, which they intend to market. He's taken the rocks from NASA for his private company, and now Anastasia wants the metal—"

"Hold on," Richard interrupted, the smile fading from his face. "My father hasn't stolen anything. And his aerospace company isn't exactly a private company. It's actually a new science outfit funded by the government. It's intended to be a partner to NASA."

Realization hit Charlie. So that was why Aerospace Infinity had lab space beneath the Smithsonian Air and Space Museum. It was funded by the US government.

And Buzz Caldwell hadn't stolen moon rocks from NASA, exactly. He was using them—perhaps without NASA's knowledge—to develop a metal to be used by the American space agency.

Even more of a reason why we can't let Anastasia get her hands on this, Charlie thought.

Then he heard shouting from behind him, and then heavy footsteps. *They're coming.*

He pushed past Richard and dove up the stairs.

"I've got to go!" he shouted. "Get help!"

He'd reached the top of the first set of stairs and turned into the second when he saw Porter and the other thug burst onto the bottom step. Richard gasped, flattening himself against the side of the stairwell as the two huge men pushed past. Charlie's eyes went wide, and he leaped upward, taking two steps at a time. They were getting closer, closer—

He flew onto the second-floor landing, nearly careening into the plaster wall directly across from him. He found his balance and continued to race forward. His eyes whirled past all the tourists, looking for an escape. So many exhibits—mechanical flying machines, space devices, a moon rover—and then ten yards ahead, something more mundane caught his gaze. A door imbedded in the wall, beneath bright red letters.

AUTHORIZED PERSONNEL ONLY.

Charlie was holding a national secret in his backpack. That seemed good enough to earn him the status of "authorized personnel."

He was breathing hard as he pinballed across the floor as fast as he could, hitting the center of the door shoulder first. The door flung inward, and he found himself leaping up another set of steps. But as he reached the top, he realized he wasn't heading to another floor of exhibits.

He found himself stepping into the guts of the ceiling. If the inner workings of the museum were pristine, clean, well orchestrated, and organized, the dark space that spread out beneath the rounded top of the building was the exact opposite. There were cables and boxes of dusty tools and wires everywhere. It looked like a junkyard.

Charlie skirted around an overturned box of tools when something caught his eye. Not a great weapon, exactly, but maybe something he could use: a pair of metal shears. He shoved them into his open backpack. Just as he took a few more steps forward, he heard a door slamming shut below and realized that Mr. Porter and his henchman had "authorized" themselves as well.

He heard a heavy, low grumble. "Charlie, your time

is running out. Here, Charlie, Charlie, Charlie. Where are you?"

Charlie had never heard Mr. Porter's voice before, and his entire body began to tremble. He picked his way forward as quietly as he could, moving around the boxes of equipment, and found himself at the edge of the metal catwalks that crisscrossed the high rounded ceiling of the main atrium. He looked down—a dizzying drop of at least fifty feet—to the atrium floor below. Then he looked directly across, through the open air of the atrium, and saw, with a start, that there was only one way out.

It was rickety and held up by metal cables.

19

"KID, DON'T DO IT. Kid!"

But Charlie was already reaching for the wire. The shears sliced through the snake of metal cable—and suddenly, Charlie was falling.

Down.

Down.

Down.

His stomach was in his mouth as the biplane plummeted, the nose dipping lower and lower. For a brief second Charlie thought he'd miscalculated, that those old wooden wings simply didn't provide enough lift to overcome the force of gravity. But then, at the last second, the nose of the plane shifted upward, and he was gliding. Not horizontal, exactly, but forward, cutting through the air like a giant version of Kentaro's paper airplane.

Wind whizzed through Charlie's hair as the biplane soared past Amelia Earhart's Lockheed Vega, hanging from similar metal wires attached to the ceiling beams. Then the plane began to jerk to the left. Charlie reached forward and grabbed what he thought was the elevator control—and the wooden stick snapped right off in his hands. He screamed. He was gliding without a stick. He grabbed the edge of the cockpit with both hands and raised himself so he could see over the nose, and saw the second-floor landing rapidly approaching. He could still make out Jeremy in the crowd, but now they were all looking in his direction, pointing and shouting. He could see the railing getting bigger and bigger, the second floor closer and closer.

Charlie closed his eyes and began to pray. The plane continued to glide downward, nose aiming straight for that railing.

Faster.

Faster.

Faster.

The nose hit with a horrible sound of crashing wood and bending metal, and suddenly Charlie was thrown forward in the cockpit. He barely held on to the edge, his feet rising all the way into the air, and still the plane skidded forward. Tourists scattered in every direction, screaming. Then the plane came to a sudden stop. Charlie opened his eyes.

He was still somehow in the cockpit, which was mostly intact, but the front of the plane had crumpled inward against the back wall of the landing. The wings to Charlie's right and left looked dented but still okay. The tail behind him was hanging through a massive hole in the railing. A few feet back, and he'd have plummeted down to the bottom. He didn't want to think about what that might have meant.

Instead, he tried to catch his breath as he quickly freed himself from the cockpit. He reached back and could feel his knapsack still strapped to his shoulders. Then he leaped out of the plane and onto the carpet. A crowd of tourists now surrounded him. Then he saw Jeremy again, off to the side.

He rushed toward his friend and didn't notice the expression on Jeremy's face until he was right up in front of him. Jeremy looked terrified. Then Charlie saw the manicured hand on Jeremy's shoulder.

Anastasia stepped out from behind Jeremy, reached forward, and grabbed Charlie's backpack off his shoulder. Charlie tried to resist, but Anastasia was too strong.

She pushed Charlie away and bent over the backpack, going to work on the zipper.

Charlie felt Jeremy pulling him farther into the crowd.

"We can't leave her with it," Charlie said, half mumbling to himself. "She can't win—"

"She's not going to win," Jeremy said.

He pulled Charlie even farther back, and Charlie could hear footsteps behind him. He turned and saw Kentaro, Marion, and Crystal running toward him. Kentaro was holding his little neon backpack out in front of him, a huge smile on his tiny face.

Charlie turned back toward Anastasia. She had gotten the zipper open, was digging inside the pack. Then her face changed. Her smile disappeared, the skin above her sunglasses wrinkled like a sun-dried grape.

She ripped her arm out of the bag. In her hand was a silver-and-gray model airplane, the words KITTY HAWK 1903 inked across the fuselage.

Anastasia looked up and saw Charlie and his friends, now twenty feet away, in the midst of a crowd of watching tourists. Her face turned bright red, and she took a menacing step toward them—

When a strong arm grabbed her by her wrist.

Standing behind her was Buzz Caldwell, tall and

handsome and wearing a leather air force flight jacket, flanked by the three NASA officials who had been watching the paper plane competition. They'd traded their notebooks for shiny badges. Along with them were two Smithsonian security guards, and behind the guards, Richard Caldwell.

As the NASA officials and security guards took Anastasia into custody, Richard found Charlie in the crowd and smiled at him. Then he gestured toward his father, and waved Charlie forward.

Charlie swallowed. Crystal patted his shoulder.

"I think you're finally going to get to meet a real live astronaut."

20

"IT WAS EVEN BETTER than I'd expected," Charlie said as he stood in front of the Whiz Kids on the train platform, waving his hands as he spoke. "Like meeting the pope, if you were Catholic. Or meeting da Vinci, if you were Marion."

"Geez," Crystal said, pulling a popsicle out of her mouth long enough to exhale. "Exaggerate much? It's not like you met Stephen Hawking. Buzz Caldwell is pretty cool, but he's just a guy who flies spaceships."

"A guy who *makes* spaceships now," Jeremy corrected. "Isn't that how this all started? He makes spaceships for one division of the government without another division of the government's permission."

Charlie laughed. A day later, and Charlie was still

trying to sort out exactly what they'd been caught up in—and how they'd managed to get through it all. Not just survive, but triumph. He could see the gold statue of that famous airplane bulging against the material of Jeremy's backpack, sitting on the bench between Kentaro and Marion. Kentaro had first tried to shove the thing into his neon pack, but of course it hadn't come close to fitting.

Even so, Charlie would never make fun of Kentaro's glowing accoutrement again. Kentaro's quick thinking when they'd run into each other in the 747 room had saved the sample from Anastasia's clutches. If Charlie had understood that look Kentaro had given him, maybe he wouldn't have attempted his dangerous escape using the biplane. Then again, Porter would have had him, and who knew what that man was capable of. Charlie was glad the NASA officials had caught him and his henchman as well, after taking Anastasia into custody for her attempted corporate espionage.

And besides, although Charlie had promised Crystal he wouldn't try anything as stupid as that again, how many other sixth graders could say they had flown a hundred-year-old biplane across the Air and Space Museum?

"Okay, he's not Hawking, but he's no slouch. And

he wasn't a thief; he was working for the government all along. And it was his word that cleared us from any trouble we might have been facing for the faked applications to the contest—or the damage we did getting away."

"The damage *you* did," Marion reminded him. "You broke a hundred-year-old biplane."

"It's being restored," Crystal said. "Anastasia's company is paying for it, with part of the fines they've been charged. And she won't be bothering anyone for a long, long time. I think it was worth it."

"Worth it?" Kentaro exclaimed. "I'm going to be in the Guinness book of world records! We won the whole competition!"

"About that," Charlie said. "You never told me how you managed that."

Kentaro closed his eyes, pressing his hands together in a prayer pose. He'd been doing that since they'd fist arrived at the train station, whenever Charlie had asked him about the winning throw. At first, Charlie had let it slide, as Marion had occupied the conversation by giving them a short tour of the main part of the station: an incredible bit of architectural history, an amalgam of neoclassicism, with elements of gold leaf and granite, and grandiose features such as a six-hundred-foot-high outer facade, and ninety-six-foot-high inner ceilings.

But now that they were down at the platform, waiting for the train that would take them back to Boston, Charlie wanted to know the truth.

"Come on, Kentaro. You've got to say something."

Charlie thought back to the awards ceremony that had taken place last night. It had been one of the happiest nights of his life. The organizers from Aerospace Infinity had lined all of his team members up on the stage of the Moretti Grand Ballroom in the hotel. Along with the huge trophy they had won, they were each awarded a gold medal engraved with their winning design, beneath the words "Nagassack Middle School." Charlie wasn't sure how the organizers had gotten the medals engraved so quickly, but Aerospace Infinity seemed to have ample funds to accomplish such feats.

Then the organizers had asked them to say a few words, and Charlie had immediately handed the mike to Kentaro—and Kentaro had simply clammed up.

"Just give me one word," Charlie said. "And I'll leave it be."

"One word?" Kentaro raised his hands, palms up. "Providence."

"That's not an explanation," Jeremy fumed. "That's a train station, right before Boston. Kentaro—"

He was interrupted by voices from the other side of the platform, more passengers coming down for the train. Charlie looked across and spotted the Worth Hooks backpacks. It only took a second more to find Kelly, standing next to Ryan by a bench overlooking the train tracks.

Charlie didn't need to tell the rest of the Whiz Kids where he was going as he headed across the platform. He could hear Crystal groaning behind him, but he ignored her. He didn't stop moving until he was right in front of Kelly and Ryan. Before either of them could say anything, Charlie reached into his backpack and withdrew an envelope.

He handed the envelope to Kelly.

"What's this?" she asked.

Ryan was looking at him suspiciously but didn't say a word. Since Charlie had bested him in the competition, Ryan had seemed to have shrunk a few sizes.

"The prize money. We talked it over, and we want you guys to have it. The organizers said it's fine for us to make the transfer."

"No way," Ryan said. "We're not charity cases."

"No, you're the rightful recipients. See, we weren't supposed to be in the contest at all. Our applications weren't filled out correctly, and we should have been disqualified. This cash prize is rightfully yours."

Kelly stared at him, trying to digest what he was saying.

"If you guys weren't supposed to be there, shouldn't Richard get the prize?"

"Richard has enough money; heck, his father owns the sponsoring company. And who knows? If you guys had been in the finals as you should have been, you might have taken him down."

Kelly and Ryan looked at each other, and then Ryan took the envelope from her and placed it in his pocket.

"Fair enough," the bigger kid said, rising up to his full height. "But next year you're going to lose to us fair and square."

"You're not going to call me a runt?" Charlie said, feeling bolder than usual. It was a good feeling, doing the right thing. He knew his parents would be proud if he told them the whole story. He still hadn't decided how much he'd reveal when he got home.

"I think you've graduated to shrimp," Ryan said. "Maybe by next year you'll be a full-size eel."

He stepped away. Charlie caught the sound of the oncoming train in the distance and turned back toward Kelly. She was smiling at him but seemed at a loss for words. Charlie wanted to tell her what he was thinking, but he wasn't sure what to say, either.

He wanted to know what the future was going to hold. Would Kelly be part of his world going forward, or were they just two paper airplanes passing in the night?

Numbers, Charlie was good at. Words, those were much harder.

Charlie only knew one thing for sure. He had an entire train ride ahead of him to find the right ones. . . .